Mrs. Alexander

Mona's Choice

Vol. I

Mrs. Alexander

Mona's Choice
Vol. I

ISBN/EAN: 9783337048037

Printed in Europe, USA, Canada, Australia, Japan

Cover: Foto ©Andreas Hilbeck / pixelio.de

More available books at **www.hansebooks.com**

MONA'S CHOICE.

VOL. I.   *a*

BY

MRS ALEXANDER,

AUTHOR OF

'THE WOOING O'T,' 'HER DEAREST FOE,'
'THE ADMIRAL'S WARD,' 'AT BAY,' 'BY WOMAN'S WIT,'
ETC., ETC.

IN THREE VOLUMES.

VOL. I.

LONDON:

F. V. WHITE & CO.,

31 SOUTHAMPTON STREET, STRAND, W.C.

1887.

EDINBURGH
COLSTON AND COMPANY
PRINTERS

CONTENTS.

MONA'S CHOICE.

MONA'S CHOICE.

CHAPTER I.

A PROPOSAL.

THE 'up' train was expected momentarily at the little junction of Galesford, from whence a line branched off to some villages and the county town.

A couple of commercial travellers, whose large neatly-strapped cases were piled on a hand-truck, stood at one end of the platform, in conversation of an amusing description, for they laughed loud and frequently.

A gentleman, covered from head to foot in a large dark ulster, walked to and fro smoking a cigar, and peering sharply into the thick mist which hid the line up to a few yards beyond the station.

The loose wrap he wore did not conceal his air of distinction. The eyes that watched so eagerly for the train, were light steely blue, his colouring was sunburnt brown, somewhat too dark for his hair and moustaches.

'Five minutes behind time,' he said, glancing at the clock over the door of the booking-office, and addressing one of the two porters who were waiting about.

'It often is, sir! You see they have often to wait at Brenton for the Altonborough passengers. It's express after this.'

'Look after my luggage! It is in the waiting-room. My name is on it—Captain Lisle—I'll be back by the six-twenty, and will not forget you.'

'Thank ye, sir! I'll take care of it right enough.'

'Two-fifteen! and here it comes!' exclaimed Captain Lisle, throwing away his cigar as the engine rushed screaming out of the dim distance, and approaching the edge of the platform he peered sharply into the carriages.

In a first-class compartment a young lady sat alone. Lisle proceeded to open the door.

'Beg pardon, sir,' said the urbane guard. 'This is a ladies' carriage—there's plenty of room in the next.'

'All right! I know the lady; she will permit me to travel a few miles in her company. Will you not?' raising his deer-stalker's cap.

'Oh, Captain Lisle!' she exclaimed, with a swift blush. 'Yes! of course.'

'Don't cram in any women or babies,' said Lisle aside quickly to the guard, pressing some coin of the realm into his hand.

'All right, sir!' significantly. 'Jump in.'

A shrill whistle, and they were off.

'I hope you will forgive my intrusion. But as I had no chance of seeing you after that telegram came, I thought I would try to say good-bye *en route.*'

He unfastened his ulster, and removed

his cap, showing a close crop of crisp brown hair, and a rather good-looking re-solute face. His keen eyes grew softer as they dwelt on his companion. She was worth looking at. Her height, even as she sat reclining in the corner of the carriage, was evidently above the average; the eyes with which she regarded him were very deep grey—large, liquid, and at the moment pathetic, almost solemn; her eyebrows were many shades darker than her hair, which admirers called golden, and detractors red, both having a fair show of reason for their opinions. Indeed the contrast between her sunny locks and her nearly black brows and eye-lashes, generally struck those who met her for the first time. Her complexion was of the purely fair description which goes with hair of her colour,—and when in repose, there was a haughty, refined ex-pression about her mouth, which, though finely formed, was not small. Her travel-ling dress of dark green cloth, simple and compact, and a velvet hat of the same colour, with a small plume of black-cock's feathers, was most becoming. As Captain

Lisle spoke, a quiet smile parted her lips, and she said gently,—

'I have nothing to forgive : you are very good to take the trouble. I fancied you were at Chillworth Castle by this time, you started so early.'

'I started at that unearthly hour to secure some private conversation with *you*.'

'Indeed!'

Again a blush, fainter this time, flitted over the lady's cheek.

'Yes. I am going to say what may perhaps offend you,—to interfere where I certainly have no right, but my sincere interest in you—my—my ardent regret that fortune should treat you so unkindly, urges me to risk making an ass of myself.'

'You puzzle me! I feel vaguely there is something I do not quite understand behind this sudden illness of my poor grandmother. Everyone seemed so sorry for me,—and Lady Mary, who is kindness itself, said she feared she had lost a great deal of money. Do tell me what you know. You always seem to me to know everything!'

'I wish I did *not* know the present state

of affairs,—and I wish you did not look as if those grand eyes of yours had been wide awake all night.

Again she smiled, a somewhat tremulous smile this time.

'Indeed I could not sleep! I was haunted by the recollection of my many quarrels with grannie,—who is really fond of me, and has been very, very good to me! I must try and make up to her for the past.'

'I can imagine that Mrs Newburgh's rule is of the iron rod order,' said Captain Lisle. 'Nor do I suppose that you are too meek a subject! I fear,' he added gravely, softly, 'that a terrible reverse awaits her—and you. The speculation in which she has invested her whole capital has come to grief,—and I fear she has lost everything.'

'How do you know?'

'Sir Robert Everard told me all particulars last night—when the other men had left the smoking-room. Mrs Newburgh's solicitor is also his. The sudden shock has been too much for her, and brought on a feverish attack.'

'Do you mean to say that we shall have no money at all?'

'I fear you will not! Everard spoke openly to me, knowing the interest I take in you, of which I hope you too are aware.'

'We have always been very good friends,' she said shyly, with quivering lips.

'Yes! and for that friendship's sake I am about to break my usual habit of not interfering with what does not absolutely concern me,—to risk the snubbing you are quite capable of administering.'

He paused, and gazed for a moment at the delicate, downcast face opposite to him, his brows contracting in a sudden frown.

'Why should I snub you?' she asked, without looking up.

'Wait till I have finished. Will you believe me when I say that I was as sleepless as yourself last night? My fancy—no, I am not an imaginative man—my experience, depicted all the hardship of your lot; for I have known difficulties—money difficulties; poverty, too, is a hundred-fold worse for a woman, a proud, delicately-nurtured woman, like yourself; and for you there is no escape, such as a man can

find in a good appointment—I hope for
one myself in India before many weeks
are over.'

'But women can work too,' she said
wonderingly. 'Why do you try to frighten
me?'

'Because I want you to seize the only
way of escape that offers.'

'Escape? How?'

'Hear me out! I am going to rush in—
probably like a fool — where angels might
hesitate to tread; but I know what life is,
and I must open your eyes. After Everard had told me all he knew, I went to my
room, and Waring, who had been dosing
over an evening paper—'

'Was *he* a confidante of our troubles
too?' she interrupted, with a slight curl of
the lip.

'He was!—that need not affect you.
Waring followed, and asked for a few
words with me. You know what a shy,
awkward fellow he is. Well, I was
amazed at his clearness and fluency—pray
hear me out. He said he came to consult
me, knowing that I had been on tolerably
intimate terms with Mrs Newburgh and

yourself all last season—in short, he con-
fessed—what I already guessed—that he
was desperately in love with you ; that he
was afraid you did not think much of him ;
and asked me if, under the circumstances,
I thought it would be good form to pro-
pose for you ! He said it cut him to the
heart, to think of your being deprived of
anything that could give you pleasure or
comfort,—I must say he spoke like a
gentleman.'

' It was very strange his consulting *you !* '
she exclaimed, with unconscious emphasis.

' I do not think it was,' he returned, with
studied composure, while he watched her
varying colour ; ' we have become rather
chums.'

'And you ?'

' I advised him to make the venture,
and I made this opportunity to advise you
to accept him.'

'Ah !' exclaimed the young lady, suddenly pressing her handkerchief to her
brow. 'There must be an east wind. Such
a sharp pain shot through my temple !
Would you draw up that window ?'

The pain was so severe that her voice

sounded unsteady.   He obeyed—and re-
suming his seat and his arguement proceeded,—

'Waring is not a bad fellow, and he is
rich, really rich, no matter if the richness
is new or old.   He is not as dull as he
seems, though dulness is no drawback to
a husband.   He adores you!—but he is
half afraid of you; you may reign supreme;
you can help your grandmother; you will
even thank me hereafter for showing you
this way to escape from the horrors of
genteel poverty, only you must *not* hesitate
in your acceptance of him.'   Lisle went on
impressively.   'He is a shy bird; if you
are not kindly, he will flutter away; you
need not affect any passion, simply promise
to be his wife.   He has a high opinion of
your integrity and honour.   He will trust
you, and when I come back after a few
years of broiling, I shall see you, I hope,
what you ought to be, a leader and an or-
nament of society, perhaps to be rewarded
for my enormous unselfishness by a renewal
of your friendship and confidence!'

While he spoke, his companion had
opened her travelling-bag, taken out a

flask of eau de Cologne, and dropped some on her handkerchief, which she applied to her forehead.

'Ah!' she said, 'it is a little better!' She raised her eyes to his with a smile, a polite smile. 'You are really very good to take all this trouble for me: it is more than I could expect! You need not exhaust yourself in persuasion: I really do not dislike Mr Waring; on the contrary, he is evidently malleable, and by no means bad-looking,— rather young perhaps, but that is a fault which corrects itself. I had no idea he thought of throwing the handkerchief to me! I am much obliged for your warning not to scare a shy bird! It is not always that a man is gifted with a figure as well as a fortune.'

She spoke with languid composure, keeping her eyes on his.

'I am very glad you take so sensible a view of my suggestion,' he returned, with slight suppressed surprise; 'as to looks, that is a matter of taste: I do not admire the "prize-fighter" style myself; but Waring is quite six or seven years older than you are! I assure you it is a relief to my mind that you deign to accept my counsel, and do not snub me for meddling.'

'That would be a bad return for your disinterested friendship. I do not think many people would imagine you capable of so Quixotic an effort to succour a damsel in distress! You do not do yourself justice, Captain Lisle! Now, do tell me something of your own plans! for I reciprocate your friendly interest, I assure you.'

'My plans,' he repeated, in a different and less steady tone. 'They are simple enough. My uncle, General Forester, has promised me an appointment on his staff. It may keep me in India the best part of my life; but I shall have leave of absence from time to time, and so keep in touch with civilisation.'

'That will be delightful! And you really have known common-place money troubles like other people?'

'Yes; very decidedly yes.'

He was feeling curiously displaced from his position of superior firmness and worldly knowledge. The unexpected acceptance of his suggestion by this fair gentle creature, who was barely nineteen, threw him off his balance.

'Then I hope they are over for ever,' she remarked, in a kindly tone. 'You must pick up a Begum in India. Yet, no! I should not like to be less bountiful than you are. I would give you a pretty, as well as a wealthy wife. Mr Waring is handsome, or rather he will develop into a handsome man. I think you have chosen well.'

'I did not choose at all. I simply did my best to induce you not to throw away a good chance. Are you serious? I do not quite understand you, Mona.'

She raised a warning finger playfully.

'As I am not, according to you, to keep my name much longer, pray let me hear it always; it is far prettier than Waring —Miss Joscelyn, if you please.'

She had grown quite animated; a faint colour replaced her extreme pallor; her large eyes sparkled; she dominated the conversation. Captain Lisle watched her closely; her manner was quite natural, while his lost the curt decision which characterised it at first. She questioned him as to how many horses Waring could keep, as to where they should live,—said she was glad he was not encumbered with landed estates, as she would like to ramble about, and much more to the same effect, half in jest. At length he looked at his watch.

'In ten minutes I must say good-bye,' he said. 'I get out at the next station, and wait for the four-fifty train to Galesford.'

'What a long tiresome wait. You really have sacrificed yourself to friendship.'

'I have,' he returned emphatically. 'I wonder if you exactly appreciate the sacrifice.'

'I do indeed.'

'May I not call and learn from your own lips how you are going on?'

'You see it is a little uncertain where you may find us. I fear they do not allow visitors at the workhouse, which may be our destination, if Mr Waring has not the goodness to charge himself with our support.'

'It is too bad that these wealthy new men get the pick of everything! Ah! here we are. Do you know, it is awfully hard to say good-bye ; I really feel a little murderous towards Waring.'

'Beware! I have taken him under my protection.'

'It is not good-bye, however; I will see you in ten days or a fortnight. Till then, *addio!*'

He pressed her hand close, she withdrew it in fierce haste; the next moment he was standing on the platform, yet another, and the train was again in motion. Miss Clifford kissed her hand with a saucy smile as she passed out of sight. The only other passenger who alighted gave up his ticket, and Lisle was left to pace the damp gravel, and think over the conversation he had just held.

'I am well out of it,' was his first thought; 'but she took my advice rather differently from what I expected. I fancied we would have had high-flown sentiment, perhaps tears and despair. I suspect I do not quite understand my fair friend. How beautifully fair she is. I did not dream she had so much pluck. By Jove! she turned my flank by her ready acceptance of my suggestion: but I fancy it was a tremendous blow, for all that! She was growing fond of me—I know it, I feel it—and *I* never was so near making a fool

of myself about any woman as about Mona
Clifford ; but it would not do ! Matrimony
is a hideous institution. Even Mona's fine
eyes, and general charm (she *is* charming !)
would lose their effect in a few years—perhaps in a few months, and I might be a
brute, or she would think me one. Women
are so terribly unpractical and illogical !
If they are worth their salt, they expect
the same constancy they bestow ; if they
are capable of making allowance, they
demand a wide margin for their own
vagaries. Now I really am loyal and
disinterested in wishing her to marry Waring. I couldn't possibly undertake her
grandmother ! She would be too expensive a luxury. Waring can afford to
pension her off ; at any rate, Mona will
clearly understand that in arranging her
future I don't count. It would have been
wrong to allow her to make any mistake
or lose a good chance. I feel I have done
my duty. I wonder if we can renew our
platonics at any future time ? Mona at
the head of a good establishment would be
quite irresistible, and Waring is one of
those happy individuals who thinks no

evil. Yes, I have certainly done the right thing for her and for myself, but there's both force and fire under her indolent softness. I wonder how she will turn out. She surely does not admire that big, rugged, overgrown schoolboy. But she may choose to assert she does, till she believes it. Women defy one's calculations. Anyhow, I did not make my early start this morning for nothing.'

Meanwhile Mona was carried deeper and deeper into the gloom of the fast closing October evening. Alone — unwatched, she let loose the reins of her self-control, and yielded to the storm of shame and despair which rent her soul.

She had indeed 'grown fond' of Lisle, after months of frequent intercourse, during which he had sought her with so much carefully-veiled assiduity — and won her confidence by a happy assumption of elder-brotherly authority, flecked with gleams of passionate admiration, which seemed to flash out in spite of himself, and were real enough. He had roused her interest, and flattered her youthful vanity—for St John Lisle was a man of good position, a favourite with fine ladies, a smart cavalry officer, of whose success in life no one had a doubt. To feel that she, a simple *débutante*, exercised an influence and attraction on such a man—was infinitely exhilarating. Lisle had been the chum and favourite brother officer of Mrs Newburgh's favourite nephew, and this was an excuse for an unusual degree of intimacy — which had increased as time rolled on, and reached a dangerous pitch during their stay at Lady Mary Everard's, the last blissful days enjoyed by Mona. Captain Lisle had begun to fear that he was going too far, and was annoyed with himself for his reluctance to draw back, when the news of Mrs Newburgh's misfortunes—the confession of young Waring, came to relieve him from the gathering difficulties of his situation. Now, a kind of lurid light from the burning of Mona's indignant heart seemed to bring out the bitter truth with stinging distinctness. She seemed to be present at that interview between Lisle and Leslie Waring. She knew, as though she had heard the words, that Waring—having noticed the understanding between her and the man who was all but her avowed lover, had asked him if they were engaged,—if it would be interfering with his (Lisle's) rights were he to offer himself to her in this crisis of her fortune. Lisle had, no doubt, disclaimed all wish to make her his wife, and coolly given his approval to Waring's pretensions. More, he had not hesitated to recommend his rival! What a reverse to the picture her fancy had hitherto presented, of Lisle vainly struggling against his love for her,—hesitating lest her relatives or herself should not think him a sufficiently good match for her,—of his ecstasy when the time came, and she permitted him to see how dear he had grown. Now behold! the time of trial came, and he was eager to hand her over to another. How could she have been so blind—so deluded? Her rage was more against herself than against him. Her long slender fingers clutched the arms of the seat with feverish force, in her agony and self-contempt. How could she have been so weak, so conceited, as to suppose that she had become all in all to such a man as St John Lisle? Yet, yet he did admire her and seek her! A hundred instances crowded on her memory which might well have misled her; important trifles which could not have occurred had he not loved her at the time. If he had, why did he change so suddenly? What had she done to forfeit the tenderness of which she was so sure? No! She was not all self-deceived. He was false, fickle, cruel— she might be less hard upon herself! Then she questioned the prudence of her own action on hearing his astounding proposal. Was it well to have played the part she did, in affecting to entertain it? Would it have been wiser and more dignified to have rebuked him for his interference, and refused to listen to his pleading? For the present, every desire was merged in her passionate wish to hide her wounds, and make Lisle believe she was as strong, as worldly, as indifferent as himself,—that his conduct did not cost her a pang. What a lesson he had taught her of her own insignificance, of the delusions she had trusted. As to poor Waring, she bestowed small consideration on his honest affection for her. Of all the house-party at Harrowby Chase, she had taken least notice of him. Their previous intercourse had consisted of a few meetings at evening parties, where he had perseveringly asked her to dance, and she had as perseveringly endeavoured to evade him. Of this he was unaware, as her manners were softly gracious, and she hated to give pain.

Now this ungraceful, shy, inarticulate young man was thrust upon her by Lisle, who had so often turned him into ridicule. Anything was good enough for a girl who was penniless and almost unprotected! It would go hard with her, she thought, while her cheeks glowed, and her heart beat fast,—very hard, before she would consent to marry him. It was almost impossible he could desire such a union himself, he always seemed so ill at ease in her presence. She wished him a better fate! Then the vision of Lisle rose before her, distinguished, self-reliant, strong, always ready to say the right thing—a man with whom the highest dared not take a liberty, and his voice vibrated again on the chords of memory, his eyes looked into hers. No! she had not deceived herself—there had been moments when St John Lisle had loved her passionately, and they had gone by for ever. Grannie might regain her little fortune, wealth might pour in upon them, but nothing could ever be to her what it had been. Between the present and the past a great gulf yawned—which nothing could fill up. And poor grannie! Mona's heart reproached her for having utterly forgotten grannie, who had been so stunned by the terrible loss which had befallen her. How her proud worldly yet sound nature would wither under the disgraces of poverty. Grannie who loved her so well, even while she tyrannised over her—she had often been rebellious, selfish, now she would try and comfort the poor old woman. She had built such hopes too on Mona's success, now everything was crumbled in the dust. The blank dreariness of the future appalled her. How could she live on—and if grannie succumbed to this attack, what was to become of her? At the thought of her isolation, of all the benefits she had received from her aged protectress, her grief and agitation found vent in a flood of tears, which lasted for many miles, yet brought relief and the calmness of exhaustion.

The Honorable Mrs Newburgh, sister of the late and aunt of the present Viscount Sunderline, had had much disappointment in her long life. Beginning with all the advantages of rank and beauty, she refused numerous excellent offers—to accept, at the mature age of thirty-five, the good-looking horsey son of a Yorkshire squire. He loved her, but he also feared her—which condition of mind led to much concealment of difficulties, and their consequent complication. Mrs Newburgh was a woman of strong will, and some business capacity, and she always held on firmly to her own small fortune. Her only son went into the army, and was killed at Inkerman. Her only daughter, who resembled her father in character, formed a strong attachment to an obscure young Scotsman, whom she met accidently in the Highlands, under somewhat romantic circumstances. Mrs Newburgh set her face against so disgraceful a union ; she dragged her pretty daughter from one Continental court to another, and finally tried to force her to marry an Englishman of high position and large fortune. This was too much, and the weak, simple, frightened girl fled to her Scotch lover. Her mother renounced her, and never saw her face again.

From this time Mrs Newburgh devoted herself to increasing her fortune, both by saving and speculating. She returned to London, and once more took her place in society.

The announcement of her daughter's death made little or no change in her way of life ; she made no attempt to communicate with the bereaved husband, and seemed to forget she had ever had a daughter. About five years later she was startled by a letter from the minister of a church in the neighbourhood of Glasgow, describing the last moments of Kenneth Craig, who had been a broken man ever since the death of his wife,

and enclosing a brief letter to Mrs Newburgh from the deceased. In it he simply
said that the pay of a bank clerk had
been too small to permit him to lay
anything by for his little girl, that his
own people were poor, that he trusted
her mother's mother would so far forgive
as not to punish the innocent, and begged
her to give the child sufficient education
to earn her bread hereafter. She was
named, he said, Mona Jocelyn, after her
mother and her uncle.

Mrs Newburgh answered this appeal by
sending for the little bright-eyed six-year-
ling, and placing her at a school specially
arranged for children whose parents were
either dead or absent. It was in the
country, and kept by a quiet motherly old
maid. For some time her grandmother
never saw Mona, but one spring, when the
child had nearly attained her tenth year,
scarlet fever broke out in the school, and
little Mona was sent off without a word of
warning to Mrs Newburgh, who had been
spending a few months in town, and was
packed up and ready to start for the
Continent.

Though dreadfully annoyed by the *contretemps*, Mrs Newburgh was struck and pleased with the improvement and promise of her granddaughter, especially as she was very like her late uncle, her reddish hair being a legacy from the plebeian Craigs. Finally she took her abroad, and placed her first at a convent school in Paris, and after in an educational establishment of a very superior description at Dresden. Here Mrs Newburgh occasionally visited her, and she remained till she was seventeen, when she went to reside with her grandmother in London; she continued to study music under the best masters, and was always present when Mrs Newburgh received. The spring before the opening of this story, she had been presented, her grandmother was well satisfied with her social success, and hoped for a brilliant marriage, when the blow fell which ruined all.

It was quite dark when Mona reached St Pancras; she was utterly weary, and profoundly still.

As a porter threw open the carriage door, a respectable foreign-looking man, somewhat tan-coloured in complexion, and pear shaped in figure, going small to the feet and spreading out roundly above, put him aside. Raising his hat, he said in German,—

'Welcome, my fraulein! I hope you are not fatigued.'

'Yes, a little, Wehner! How is my grandmother?'

'Better, my fraulein! but weak! ah, very weak. She is looking anxiously for you. If you get into the cab, I will find your baggage.'

CHAPTER II.

ANOTHER.

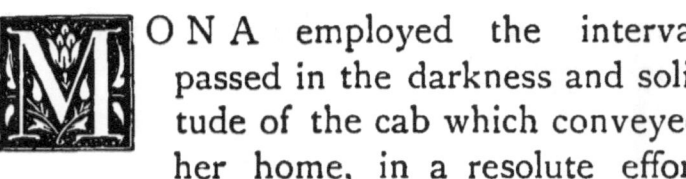

ONA employed the interval passed in the darkness and solitude of the cab which conveyed her home, in a resolute effort to regain her self-possession. She dreaded to meet grannie's keen, observant eyes; she dreaded too, the mood which her severe losses would most probably have induced. Mrs Newburgh, though generally keeping herself well in hand, had her tempers, and Mona became a favourite chiefly because she was not frightened by them. She was far from realising as yet the total loss which had befallen.

The door was opened by Mrs Newburgh's maid, a very important person, with whom

Mona had not unfrequent differences of opinion. Her face was expressive of ill-temper and disgust.

'Mrs Newburgh has been worriting herself and everyone else because she fancies you are late, miss,' was her salutation.

'I do not think I am, Hooper!'

'I daresay not; only you see she is all wrong about time—a minute or an hour, it's all one to her. I never thought you would see her alive. After she read about that cruel deceitful, swindling company in the paper, she sent off Mr Wehner for Mr Macquibble. After they had talked a bit, the bell rung sharp; I was called, and there was Mrs Newburgh in a dead faint. I thought she would never come to. We called the doctor and put her to bed, but she had three more faints before night. Then we telegraphed for you, miss. Nothing would keep her in bed this afternoon,—she got up and dressed.'

'Poor, dear grannie! I will go to her at once!'

'Won't you have a cup of tea first, miss? you are looking dreadful bad!'

' No, thank you, Hooper!'

She went quickly upstairs to her grandmother's room, and having paused for a second at the door, went in softly.

Mrs Newburgh sat at a writing-table covered with letters, papers, account and cheque books—some notes and gold at her right hand. She was wrapped in a morning-gown of dark red cashmere, and her grey hair was neatly arranged under her lace cap; but Mona was startled by the ghastliness of her face. Mrs Newburgh had borne the wear and tear of time well, and having accepted her age without a struggle for youthful appearance, did not look her seventy-six years. Now she might have been a hundred. Her cheeks seemed thinner and more sunken; wrinkles had come about her mouth, the muscles of which were relaxed into a downward curve; her face was deadly white; her keen dark eyes were dim and frightened; the hands which lay on the table were yellow and tremulous. Mona's heart thrilled with pity at the sight of such a wreck.

' Oh, grannie!—dear grannie!' was all she could say, coming quickly to her, and gathering up the cold, withered hands into her own, as she kissed her cheek.

The old lady clasped her almost convulsively.

' I thought you would never come,' she whispered brokenly. ' Do you know that everything is gone ?—everything ! We cannot stay here. This is the last money I can call my own '—and she freed one hand to clutch the gold and notes. ' I don't seem able to understand the figures or anything ! You will not leave me, Mona ? Hooper is so cross that '— gathering force by a supreme effort, and speaking with something of her natural decision—' I should in any case dismiss her ; for me all is over. I am too old to struggle any longer. I have fought a brave fight, but Fate is against me. Mona, my child, can you forgive me for losing the little fortune I intended for you ? Somebody told me I ought to draw out of that company—I forget who —I forget all the names ; but I thought I might wait a little longer—the interest was so high—and I have beggared you ! Can you forgive ?'

'Forgive you!' cried Mona, sinking on her knees and clasping her arms round her trembling grandmother. 'What have I to forgive? Rather let *me* pray your forgiveness for my want of obedience and submissiveness! Where should I be but for you? I owe you everything! Send away Hooper—I will be your maid, your nurse, your servant,—anything that can help or comfort you!'

'Foolish, hasty child!' murmured Mrs Newburgh, laying her hand tenderly on the young head pressed against her. 'I believe you love me a little.'

And the poor, deathlike face brightened for a moment, as the sceptical, world-hardened woman caught a breath of the divine consolation human love alone can give, and which all the kingdoms of this world and the glory of them cannot replace.

'I do love you, dear! I will do whatever you wish; and do not be so cast down—something will be arranged for us. We can go away and live in the country, then we shall not want expensive dresses, and—'

'You little know!—you little know!'

murmured Mrs Newburgh. 'Thank God,
I have few debts! I think I have paid
every one—intending to go abroad for
some months. This has been an expensive year, and there was no time for you to
make a good alliance. No time—no time!'

'But, grannie dear, you do not know
what prince in disguise I may captivate,'
said Mona, rising and drawing a chair
beside her. 'Penniless girls marry often.'

She would have said anything to cheer
her.

'Ay! but no jewel looks well if it is not
well set. Men may not want money with
their brides, but they are almost always
repulsed by mean surroundings. I see no
hope anywhere. None—none!'

There was a long pause. Then Mrs
Newburgh began with an effort to explain
how matters stood. It was pitiable to
hear how she lost the thread of her nar-
rative and struggled to regain it—how she
called people by wrong names, and repeated
herself over and over again,—insisted on
having the money counted out before her,
and strove to separate it into different por-
tions. At last she perceived her own in-

ability to convey her meaning, and leant suddenly back in her chair.

'Everything fades from me,' she said; 'yet I am not imbecile.'

'No, no! dearest grannie! This confusion is only from physical weakness. Do not try yourself any more. I will write to Mr Oakley—to your solicitor—to come here to-morrow; he will put things in order, and tell me what we ought to do. Let me lock up all these papers and the money, and give you some dinner or tea or something. Thinking will do us no good. To-night I will tell you all about Lady Mary and my visit, then I will sit by you till you are asleep. Hooper shall put the chair bed beside yours. I shall sleep here to-night.'

'It would be best,' murmured Mrs Newburgh, gladly resigning herself to her grand-daughter's guidance. 'I do not want much; but for you,—ah, Mona! it is hard! You must pay Hooper and send her away, and Wehner too: we want no men-servants now.'

．　．　．　．　．　．　．　．

The explanations of Mrs Newburgh's

trusty solicitor were indeed a revelation to Mona. The mysteries of the stock market were unfolded to her wondering gaze ; and she learned that besides the considerable sum absolutely paid on the purchase of shares, there was a terrible liability in the shape of ' calls ' to the full value of these shares ; and as a banking business was connected with the gold mine association, Mrs Newburgh's whole property was subject to the demands of depositors, and that she could not call a farthing her own.

The house in Green Street having been bought by her, Mr Oakley advised Mrs Newburgh remaining in it till obliged to turn out, as she was rent free. He was most useful in paying and dismissing the servants. The German major-domo, who had been for many years with Mrs Newburgh, begged to be allowed to remain till his mistress left—without wages ; it was, he said a bad season to find another engagement, and he thought he could be useful to the ladies, even while looking out for a situation, and so he proved himself.

While these changes were going on,

Mona was profoundly anxious about her grandmother. At times she was keen, eager, fully alive to what was going on; then a cloud would gather over her poor brain, and things seemed to slip from her. She could not bear Mona out of her sight, and was reluctant to let any other relatives approach her. When urged by Oakley to acquaint her nephew, Lord Sunderline, with the state of her affairs, she asked sharply what good that would do?

'He has little enough for himself, and never forgave me for adopting Mona.'

'But, my dear madam, some steps must be taken to provide for the future.'

'I wish Nature would provide for me,' returned Mrs Newburgh, with a deep sigh; 'I am a helpless encumbrance now.'

'I am sure no one else thinks so,' said the solicitor soothingly. 'Is there not some balance at your bankers that you might place in—say Sir Robert Everard's hand, just to secure some ready money?'

'I will see; I will look into my accounts, but for the present I am too tired to discuss anything further.'

.   .   .   .

Mrs Newburgh could not, however, complain of any want of interest on the part of her numerous friends and acquaintances ; she was overwhelmed with letters of condolence, of inquiry, of the most impossible suggestions.

These were generally read aloud by her grand-daughter, or as much of them as she would listen to. Sometimes she would grow feverish over attempted calculations ; sometimes she would sit for hours deadly silent.

The fourth day after her return home, Mona was as usual in attendance on her grandmother, and making out a list of such necessaries as they might take with them, when two letters arrived by the second delivery. One was from Sir Robert Everard —a distant cousin of Mrs Newburgh's— and offered her a cottage which used to be occupied by one of the curates of the parish, suggesting that she might remove some of her furniture there before the final crash came, and adding much kindly counsel. The other was in a big, firm but unknown hand. Mona turned to the signature—it was 'Leslie Waring.' She had almost forgotten him in the painful excitement of the last few days, though the bitter remembrance of Lisle's advice never left her. Every night when she had read or softly talked her grandmother to sleep, when all was still and dark, she lived over again the fiery ordeal of that conversation in the train, and looked, shuddering, at the dreary, lonely future, through which she must do battle alone. To whom could she turn, on whom could she lean, when the man who seemed to hang on her words— whose eyes spoke the warmest devotion, shrank from her at the first mutterings of the storm? But as to when Mr Waring would declare himself, or whether he ever would, she gave no thought. Now the momentous question on which she would be called to decide stared her in the face, and filled her soul with fear and disgust.

'I cannot read this letter to you, grannie; could you read it yourself?'

'Why? What is it?'

'It is marked private, and is, I see, from Mr Waring; do you remember him?'

'Yes, I do! Give it to me. Where are my glasses?'

Mona sat and watched the haggard, hopeless face, as her grandmother perused the lines, gradually growing less drawn, less desponding, while her own heart sank lower and beat faster.

'Thank God,' murmured Mrs Newburgh at last, heaving a deep sigh as she laid down the letter; 'all is not quite lost yet.' Mona did not speak. 'Mona! read it,' she continued; 'I suppose you know the contents; read it, I say,' repeated Mrs Newburgh impatiently.

Mona took it and read with nervous rapidity,—

'DEAR MRS NEWBURGH,—I venture to trouble you with a letter, because I have twice tried in vain to see you or Miss Joscelyn. I feel it is awkward and difficult to approach the subject on which I am about to address you, when I have had so few opportunities of making myself known, but I earnestly hope you will exonerate me from the charge of presumption, and that Miss Joscelyn will not refuse to let me explain myself to her personally. If I dare to be somewhat premature, it is because I be-

lieve I might be of some use in the present
crisis, were I so fortunate as to be accepted
by the lady to whose hand I aspire.   Indeed, under any circumstances, I should be
proud to be of the smallest service to you,
and beg to assure you that I am ready to
meet your wishes in all ways.   Looking
anxiously for your reply.—I am, yours
faithfully,   LESLIE WARING.'

There was a short silence when Mona
ceased.

'A very good letter,' said Mrs Newburgh, with a little gasp, looking with
pitiful, imploring eyes at her grandchild.

'I wonder if he composed it himself,'
observed Mona quietly.

'My child, could you make up your
mind to marry this young man? I have
noticed his admiration of you.   He writes
like an honest gentleman.   Let me have
the comfort of knowing that you have
escaped the ills of poverty.'

'Oh, grannie, it is a tremendous price
to pay for safety!   Mr Waring may
be a better man than I deserve; but I
do not care for him.   He seems to me

an awkward big boy, — dull and un-
formed.'

Mrs Newburgh sighed deeply, and
closed her eyes.

'I leave it to yourself. I am such a
failure, I dare not urge my advice on anyone. I was too urgent with your mother.
Do as you will, Mona.'

'Oh! what ought I to do?' exclaimed
Mona. 'It is awful to think of spending one's whole life with a man to whom
you are indifferent; it is cruel to refuse
the only efficient help for you, dear
grannie.'

'Think of yourself—yourself only; as
for me, I—' her voice grew feeble, her
words inarticulate, her head fell back, and
to Mona's dismay she became insen-
sible.

All other considerations were forgotten
in the efforts to recover her. The faithful
Wehner went swiftly for the doctor, who
happened to have returned from his morning rounds and came at once.

'It's a bad business these repeated
attacks,' he said to Mona, after he had
seen his patient. 'Her nerves are all

wrong. Her mind *must* be kept at ease somehow. Get her out of this!'

'We expect Sir Robert Everard the day after to-morrow, and then we shall decide what to do,' faltered Mona.

'The sooner the better, my dear young lady,' returned the doctor, who knew Mrs Newburgh well. 'She will go off in one of these attacks, or her mind will become seriously impaired. A woman of her age can hardly stand the shock of such a reverse. Keep her very quiet; she seems drowsy—the best thing for her is a good sleep; do not leave her; she must be watched. I will look in this evening about seven.'

Mona's thoughts were sorely troubled as she kept watch at her grandmother's bedside. She knew that her marriage with Waring—or even the prospect of it, would be the best restorative for her only friend, the woman who had been a mother to her, who had saved and worked to amass the means of independent existence for her, who had loved her after her own hard but tenacious fashion. She recalled, with a swelling heart, her grand-

mother's watchful economy, her self-denial
in all things necessary to herself. She did
not doubt that any niggardliness towards
her grandchild was for her future good.
How wise and judicious she had been in
her guidance of their lives. If she had
shown too strong a tendency to marry her
grand-daughter as soon as possible to the
highest bidder, she only acted according
to her lights—to the creed of her world
and her period. Was it well for Mona to
refuse the means of giving her a longer
and brighter spell of life? Dare she incur
the responsibility of her possible death?
What would she gain—what had she to
hope for, in an unmarried life, that she
should reject this kind-natured man who
only asked leave to devote his fortune to
her service. With the tendency of youth
to believe in the perpetuity of the present,
she thought that love with her was over
for ever. She could never believe anyone
again. She was not angry with Lisle, so
much as disenchanted ; her anger was
more against herself, for her weakness and
credulity.

A soft tap at the door attracted her at

tention ; she rose and cautiously opened
it.

'Madame Debrisay is below, wanting
to speak with you, ma'am,' said the woman
who had replaced both cook and house-
maid.

'I should like to see her ; could you
stay for a little with Mrs Newburgh while
I go downstairs.'

'Yes'm. I think Mr Wehner is just
come in. I will ask him to answer the
door, and come back directly.'

Having given a few directions, Mona
ran downstairs lightly, well pleased to have
a confidential talk with her visitor.

Madame Debrisay had been her greatest
friend when she was at school in Paris.
There she had been the junior music mistress, and Mona had been immensely attracted by the kindliness and good-humour
of the hard-working teacher.

When Mona left, Madame Debrisay
moved to London, and with Mrs Newburgh's help contrived to make a good
connection as a music and singing mistress.
She gave Mona lesssons, or rather assisted
her in practising for an expensive master,

and continued her warmest admirer and
devoted friend. Both Madame Debrisay
and her late husband the Captain were
British subjects, being natives of the
Emerald Isle, but she deemed it wise to
pose as a foreigner, with a view to obtain-
ing a better position in her profession; and
possessing dramatic instincts, she played
her part artistically, speaking English with
a foreign accent, and even brokenly at
times, a proceeding she justified by assert-
ing that the late Debrisay and herself were
really French, being descended from the
Huguenots who had fled from the persecutions of Louis the Fourteenth.

The small fireless dining-room looked
so dismal and dark that chill November
afternoon, that Mona called Wehner to
light the gas, that she might see her
friend's face.

'Oh! me dear child '(sounded like choild)
—her native accent came out when she
was much moved, ' I have only just come
back from the sea side, and heard some bad
news, so I ran round to get at the truth
from yourself.'

' You cannot have heard anything worse

than the truth, Deb,' returned Mona.
'Poor grannie has lost everything. I
scarcely know what is to become of us.'

'*Dieu des Dieux!* you don't say so.
Don't tell me you have to face the black
death! for that's what poverty is. There
is no misfortune like it, and *I* know. Oh,
my dear—my jewel, can you see no way
out of it?'

'No; no way I should care to try.'

'Ha! there is a blink of hope somewhere
then? How is your dear good grandmother? How will she ever bear "going
down?"'

'She is very unwell and weak: I am
quite frightened about her.'

'And no wonder!'

Madame Debrisay untied her veil, and
sat down with a despondent air. She was
a plump woman, under middle height, with
dark eyes, iron-grey hair, a decidedly
turned-up nose, a wide, smiling mouth,
which was rarely quite closed over her
beautifully white teeth.

'Tell me all about everything.'

And Mona explained as far as her
imperfect knowledge permitted.

'Those promoters and scamps who get
up these companies to rob and plunder the
world ought to be hung! I know the
cruel way they work. You pay a few
pounds on each share, and all goes swim-
ingly for a bit, and then you take more,
and chuckle over the good income they
bring in, never doubting that their value
will double by-and-by; then comes the
crash, and you find all you possess clawed
up by those villains—and I'm afraid they
will make a clean sweep of poor dear
Mrs Newburgh's money, that she was so
fond of. Not but that she was generous
and kind too,' added Madame Debrisay,
hastily correcting herself.

'I am afraid they will! I try hard to
think what will become of us,—of what I
ought to do,' returned Mona, with a deep
sigh. 'I fear I am very useless. What
can I do to earn money?'

'You earn money! Why, it is hard
enough for those who have been trained
for work to find the means of existence;
and you—' here she found her handkerchief
necessary. 'That I should live to hear
you speak of such a thing! Not that the

work itself is hard—an idle life is the
worst of all!—it's the looking for it, and
the failures, and the waiting. No, my
dear, you must make up your mind and
marry some nice rich man.'

Mona laughed, but her laugh was not
merry.

'Dear Deb! you are as imaginative as
ever! Nice rich men are not plentiful,
nor are they ready to marry penniless girls.'

'Yes, Englishmen are. And you must
not be too hard to please. I remember
that night I went to Mrs Vincent's *soirée
musicale*, to play the accompaniments, there
was a fine, elegant, *distingué* man talking
to you, and watching you. I asked you
about him after, but you would only
laugh. You told me his name, but I
cannot think of it.'

'Mrs Vincent's party,' said Mona, blush-
ing. 'There was a crowd of very polite
gentlemen there,' she added evasively.

How well she remembered that blissful
evening—what a thrill of pain the mention
of it sent through her heart.

'Ay! but this one was more than polite.
He was a Captain—Captain Lisle, that's

it. Now, why wouldn't you take him?'

'Because he never asked me for one thing,' said Mona, nerving herself to speak lightly and smile carelessly. 'I suspect he is a man who wants a great deal of money, and has very little.'

'Oh! he isn't badly off! I know they were talking of him, and of a rich widow who wanted to marry him, and Mrs Vincent said he was too independent to be a fortune-hunter,—that he had six or seven hundred a year, to say nothing of his pay.'

'That is not being rich,' returned Mona, trying to evade the subject, but making a mental note of the fact that Lisle was *not* poor; then a sudden impulse prompted her to confide her difficulties to her shrewd, sympathising friend. 'But I am in a painfully undecided state of mind about a really rich man who has written to my grandmother asking leave to " pay his addresses to me," as old-fashioned people say.'

'Thank God!' exclaimed Madame

Debrisay devoutly. 'And will he do, dear?'

'A week ago I should have said certainly not! Now,' her voice broke, 'when I think of poor grannie's wistful eyes when I hesitated, I feel I ought not to refuse! Then she fainted away, as if she could bear no more. How can I rob her of her last hope, I, who have been so much trouble? And yet, the idea of marrying this man is —horrible.'

Her lips trembled, the long pent-up despair and anguish of her heart would be no longer controlled. Covering her face, she burst into tears, struggling hard to suppress the bitter sobs which would come.

'Why, my darlin', is he a monster?' asked Madame Debrisay, dismayed.

'No—o,' said Mona, when she could articulate. 'He is a good-natured, well-meaning young man, rather tiresome and heavy. I used to dance with him last season, and he called here a few times. Then he was staying at the Chase (oh! it was such a pleasant party!), but he did not seem to notice me much. Then this

morning came a letter from him expressing a wish to marry me.'

'Small blame to him!' ejaculated Madame Debrisay. 'And are you quite sure
he is rich ?'

'I know nothing about it, but grannie
seems quite sure.'

'Is he a fright ?'

'Well, no. Lady Mary thinks him rather
handsome; but I have seen some quite
ugly men I thought better looking.'

'I'll ask you just one question more;
don't think I want to pry into your heart,
—but, do you love anyone else ?'

'No, Deb, I do not,' said Mona, believ-
ing she spoke the truth, and meeting her
friend's eyes steadily.

'Then, my dear, you marry him out of
hand, and turn your back on misery. That
man is the right sort: he stands by you in
the time of trouble; before a year is out,
you will be ready to eat him—mark my
words!'

'If I could hope to do so!' said Mona,
with a deep sigh.

'Ah! Mona, my dear child! it's better
to find love growing after marriage than

to watch it die out, and rake the ashes
together, and try and try to keep it alight,
and burn up your own heart in vain!
Take this honest soul, and make him
happy, and you'll be happy yourself.   A
good man is not to be found every day.
As for the sort of poetical, graceful, mutual
love young creatures dream about, I'll not
say it never exists, but it is as scarce as
blue roses.   My dear, for one heart that
can give it, there are a thousand made
of coarser stuff.   You marry this man,
and give your poor dear grandmother a
bright sunset before she goes.   What's
his name?' concluded Madame Debrisay
abruptly.

'Leslie Waring—'

'Hem! I never heard it before—and
I hear a lot of gossip.   Is he a new
man?'

'I fancy he is, but I know very little
about him.'

'You are looking ill, very ill, dear.   I
suppose you never go out?   No?   I
thought not.   Now my pupils have not
come to town yet, so while I have time
I'll come over and stay with Mrs New-

burgh, so that you may take a little walk;
—nothing like fresh air for keeping the
nerves in tune.'

'Thank you very much—and now I am
afraid I must go back to grannie. Have
you changed your rooms yet? How have
you been? I am so selfish about my own
troubles that I have forgotten to ask you.'

'I am as fresh as the flowers in May.
I was dead beat at the end of the season
—but it was a good one—so I went to
Southsea to stay with the Winklemans.
He is bandmaster to one of the regiments
there. *She* is a sweet little Frenchwoman,
I knew her in Paris. I had a very nice
time, and it freshened me up. I have
found very good rooms in Westbourne
Villas, and cheaper than what I had.
I have a big bedroom, and a nice par-
lour. The woman of the house is a
widow, and glad to have a permanent
tenant. You'll come to see me, dear,
one day?'

'Oh, yes! It is such a comfort to talk
to you, and tell you things. You dear,
good Deb! All I have told you is a dead
secret.'

'Of course it is. I know I talk a good deal, but I never let out anything I was trusted with. Now, God bless you. Mind you write me word to-morrow that you have agreed to marry Mr Waring. There's my address. Ain't my new cards pretty?'

CHAPTER III.

YES.

SLEEP partially restored Mrs Newburgh ; but next morning her grand-daughter observed that she was restless and watchful —especially of herself. The doctor forbade her leaving her bed, as the weather was extremely cold, and a chill might be fatal.

When Mrs Newburgh's *toilette de lit* was made, and her pillows properly arranged, Mona took her work and sat down beside her—feeling quite sure that her grandmother was making up her mind to speak. This change in the somewhat abrupt, domineering old woman touched her—it was such a confession of utter defeat.

'You will be glad to see Sir Robert, grannie,' she began. 'He will give us some good advice.'

'Not half so good as Mr Oakley can,' returned grannie querulously. 'He is a mere country gentleman, and nothing can save me from total ruin. What troubles me is that letter of Mr Waring's. It ought to be answered. I think I could manage to write, if you bring me the large blotting-book.'

'Yes, of course, it ought to be answered,' returned Mona, very gravely.

'But how?' asked Mrs Newburgh. 'If you refuse to see him, all is over. If you consent, it implies acceptance.'

'Not quite, grannie. I have been thinking all night long what I ought to do—what I can do. It seems impossible to decide. I believe I could make up my mind better if I had some conversation with Mr Waring. I am so indifferent, that I do not think his presence would even confuse me.'

'Do see him, Mona; your feelings

may be touched when you find yourself
face to face with a man who sincerely
loves you. And this man has proved
his sincerity.'

'Or his determination to gratify his
whim, cost what it may,' added Mona.

'You have no right to impugn his
motives. Great as my desire is to see
you lifted safe above the bitter flood of
poverty, I would not urge you to a
repulsive marriage.'

'Forgive me, grannie. I am ungracious, selfish. If I marry Mr Waring,
I will do it cheerfully.'

She rose and brought the writing
materials. 'I will see him, but I do
not promise to accept him, unless—'

'Let him plead his own cause,' interrupted Mrs Newburgh, stretching out
her hand for pen and paper. 'He will
induce you to take a different view, I
am sure.' With difficulty she traced a
few lines, excusing their brevity on the
score of illness, and asking him to call
on the following day, when Miss Joscelyn
would receive him. 'You must address
it, dear. He does not know your hand.'

'It is of no consequence,' said Mona; removing the writing materials; and taking out an envelope, she sat down to direct it.

'It is not natural, Mona, to be so cold and indifferent. Yet I have not detected any liking on your part for any other man, except, indeed—'

'No, no,' interrupted Mona quickly. 'I have no preference for any one, rest assured, dear grannie.'

'Then, Mona, you will love young Waring when he is your husband.'

'Oh! yes, I daresay I shall. Now, grannie, I am going to read you the paper, try and listen—it may rest your brain a little.'

'I will, Mona, I will, because you have given me a little hope.'

The rest of the dull, drear November day, Mona moved slowly perhaps, but firmly, as if keenly alive to the work she had to do. But side by side with her clear perception of duty and responsibility, was another sense of coming pain and sacrifice. Were she alone, with only self to provide for, she could launch herself upon the ocean of life—fearlessly, if hopelessly. But she must not desert her grandmother! and if she could provide for her in no other way, she was almost bound to provide for her by 'accepting service'—so she termed it in her own mind—with Mr Waring. If only—it was not to be marriage.

Late in the afternoon a card was brought her. 'Captain St John Lisle,—th Hussars.' She thought an instant, pencilled a line on it, 'So sorry! I cannot leave Mrs Newburgh,' and sent it back to him.

This incident was in Waring's favour.

'I should like to tell him that I am engaged to his *protégé*, when we next meet,' she thought. 'Yet how base it is to be thus influenced by pique against one man, in my acceptance of another,—another who perhaps really loves me, for I suppose I shall accept him. As George Elliot says, "One may rave upon the heights, but you know that your persistent self awaits you on the plain," the terrible dead level of necessity to which I am fast sinking. But, right or wrong, I will pose to Captain Leslie as a hard-

headed worldling. He shall not pity me,
or suspect my contemptible weakness.
He shall not fancy he was in such danger
of being dragged down by my misfortunes
that it was necessary to pass me on to
someone else. Could I have betrayed
my feelings so completely, that he should
think it necessary to take decided measures
for self defence? Yet how utterly I believed in him! Was I self-deceived, or—
but I will *not* think any more of myself,
and my folly, my contemptible folly! I
ought to forget self altogether. It is the
best way to be happy. Ah! shall I ever
be happy again?'

Captain Lisle was not the only visitor
to Green Street that day. Late in the
afternoon, Sir Robert Everard was announced.

'I cannot see him,' murmured Mrs
Newburgh. 'You must go, Mona—explain how incapable I feel.'

Sir Robert was a thorough country
gentleman. He seemed to bring an
atmosphere of the woods and fields with
him into the chill, dull dining-room, which
had a deserted air. A middle-aged,

middle-sized man, plump and rosy, with pepper - and - salt - coloured mutton - chop whiskers, looking always as if he had come fresh from a bath. His shirt fronts were the snowiest, his clothes the glossiest, his voice had a mellow ring in it, which atoned for the loud, authoritative key in which he usually spoke.

'Well!' he exclaimed, taking Mona's hand in one of his, and patting it with the other, 'how is the poor grannie? I protest I never was more cut up than when I found how desperately she has been swindled! She would stick to the ship, in spite of all that Oakley or I could say. The few solvent shareholders backed out some time ago, and the rest are mostly men of straw, so they'll not leave Mrs Newburgh a rap.'

'Poor dear grannie is very, very miserable, Sir Robert. It is curious that so clever a woman should have believed in what many of her friends and advisers doubted?'

'She was always obstinate, my dear, devilish obstinate! However, I have a bit of good news. A friend of mine wants

to buy the house. He will give a decent
sum too ; and I want your grandmother to
convey the money to me for you, or some
legal jugglery of that kind. Go, ask her
if she will be able to see me and Oakley
to-morrow, that we may settle about it.
It will be a something between you and
want.'

'I will go and tell her,' said Mona,
hastening away. 'Will it be enough to
save me from the necessity of marrying
anyone?' she thought.

Sir Robert Everard put his hands in his
pockets, and paced the room whistling
softly.

'Poor old soul! won't last long, I daresay. The girl will marry: no doubt of
that ; she is deuced handsome—a well-bred
one too. Would run smooth and easy
in double harness. Fellows are cooler and
more cautious than they were in my days,
but there are plenty of rich ones who
might indulge themselves in a handsome,
penniless wife.'

'My grandmother will be glad to see
you to-morrow at twelve,' said Mona,
coming back.

'All right; just sit down and write a line to Oakley, asking him to meet me here. We will have a consultation, then we'll see what is best to be done; we must secure whatever money Mrs Newburgh gets for the house from the claws of the liquidators. Lady Mary wants her,—both of you—to come down to the Chase. I am going to shoot in Ross-shire; Eveline comes with me. The other two are going for a month with their aunt to Biarritz; so you will be quite quiet. A change will do your grandmother a lot of good, and set her up again, hey?'

'Thank you so much; it would indeed. I am afraid it will be some time before she can be moved,' returned Mona, who shrank from the idea of visiting the Chase again.

'You would be all the better for being turned out to grass yourself, my dear,' he resumed kindly. 'It's hard lines for a young thing like you to be plunged into such trouble. Why, you are not as old as Eveline. I suppose grandmamma is not in the sweetest temper;

—a little hard in the mouth just now,
eh ? '

' Oh, no, Sir Robert; she is an angel.
She seems to have lost faith in herself;
she has not the force to insist on anything; it breaks my heart to see her so
pitifully gentle.'

' She must be badly hit. I am awfully
sorry for her—for both of you. Just write
that, my dear, will you ? I'll post it as
I go along. And I must leave you now.
I am going to dine with Rivers. You
remember Rivers who was at the Chase
when you were with us ? Rich old dog—
won't spend a penny on anything but
his dinners—they are first-rate. He is
a crotchety old sinner; seldom goes to
any one's house. Lady Mary was rather
proud of his staying nearly a week with
us ; but he did not get such dinners in
my house as he has in his own.'

Sir Robert Everard talked on in his
kindly, easy way while Mona wrote the
note.

Mr Oakley obeyed the summons.
Mrs Newburgh, revived by her new
hopes, was up and dressed when Sir

Robert and the solicitor arrived. She had, with the help of Wehner's arm, descended to the drawing-room ; but she looked like the ghost of her former self.

Then ensued a long, melancholy discussion, at which Mrs Newburgh insisted her grand-daughter should be present, and from which the latter gathered that it was of no use endeavouring to save anything out of the wreck—that whatever the unfortunate shareholders possessed must pass into the clutches of the company's creditors ; a call had already been made, and would be followed by others, until all was swallowed up. It was therefore deemed more prudent for Mrs Newburgh to reside in the house she had bought, than to move to another for which she would have to pay rent. Her income had of course been narrowed to a miserable eighty or ninety pounds a year, and even on that she could not long count.

' You see, Mona, the condition to which we are reduced,' said Mrs Newburgh, when their friendly counsellors, with grave faces and kindly-expressed sympathy, had withdrawn. ' I purposely asked you to be present at this conference, that you might understand the true state of the case. I leave you to draw your own conclusions. No, dear, do not re-open the discussion. I trust to your own common-sense and right feeling. I am quite exhausted. Ring for Wehner to help me to my room. I can see no one else to-day—*no* one— remember, Mona.'

Thus cut off from remonstrance, Mona felt she was left to her fate and Mr Waring; grannie was resolved to leave the decision—the responsibility—to her.

Mrs Newburgh had not long returned to her own room, and had just taken some refreshment, when Mr Waring's card was brought. A strong feeling of humiliation and disgust rose in Mona's heart; the calm indifference of which she boasted the previous day failed her at the moment of trial.

' Do not keep the poor young man waiting,' said Mrs Newburgh.

' It is frightful, having to go deliberately to listen to an offer of marriage!' cried Mona, starting up and walking to the window instead of the door.

' I thought you would not mind.'

' I *thought* so ; but I will go, dear grannie.'

She came back quickly, kissed the old woman's cheek, and disappeared.

Mona went rapidly downstairs, and straight into the dining-room, without allowing herself to pause for a moment — half frightened, half angry, at her own faintness of spirit.

Mr Waring stood on the hearthrug. He was not so tall as Lisle ; his broad shoulders and rather short neck further diminished his height. He was built more for strength than grace, and though not fat, was, it must be admitted, fleshy. His hair was dark, almost black, abundant and wavy, and his broad, good-humoured face was redeemed from absolute plainness by a pair of fine soft dark brown eyes. He was in general ruddy and fresh-looking, but the excitement, indeed it may be said the terror of the moment, had blanched his cheeks, till he met Mona's eyes, when he blushed furiously.

She hesitated after she had crossed the threshold, and closed the door, standing tall, stately, infinitely sad, in the simplest morning dress of black silk and cashmere she possessed, a lace scarf pinned round her throat with an old-fashioned brooch, her bright hair turned loosely back surmounting her fair pale face like an aureole.

'I am so much, so very much obliged to you for seeing me!' exclaimed Waring, starting forward to take her hand, which he shook nervously, and dropped immediately. Mona murmured something, he did not hear what, and sat down beside the fire.

Waring resumed his position on the hearthrug. An awful pause ensued. Mona gazed at the glowing coals, and thought of Lisle's expressive voice and perfect, easy self-possession. Waring cudgelled his brain for some suitable phrase to open the dreaded yet longed for conversation. The result was a restless change of attitude, and the words. 'Awful nasty weather.' His voice was strong and harsh. 'I hope you took no cold on your journey to town.'

It was an unlucky allusion.

'Not a cold; I had a slight *chill*,' returned Mona, who had some sense of humour.

She raised her eyes as she spoke, and meeting his, could not restrain a kindly smile, feeling no little sympathy with his uneasiness and evident sense of difficulty.

'You are amused, I daresay,' he cried, his power of speech unlocked by the magic of her smiling eyes; 'you *must* be amused, to hear me blundering like an idiot about the weather, when my heart and mind are filled with hope and fear. Tell me, Miss Joscelyn, did Mrs Newburgh show you my letter?'

'She did.'

'And will you—will you let me tell you how awfully I was taken with you the very first time I ever saw you at that Richmond dinner Lady Mary Everard gave last year,—before you were presented, you know?'

'Were you there?' asked Mona dreamily.

At that dinner she had first met Lisle. He had not spoken to her, but she had even then felt a degree of attraction to him which surprised her, and he had remarked her—or—said so.

'Oh, I don't suppose you saw me. I never *can* push. Young Everard and some other fellows were round you all the time; but I have thought of you ever since. Do you know, last season's balls were the first I ever went to. I thought they were all rot. I like the racing set better. I used to go only for the chance of meeting you,—and you would scarcely ever dance with me. To be sure, I am a stupid beggar about dancing.'

A pause.

'I think I always gave *some* dances,' said Mona, rather at a loss what to reply.

'Oh, you were always civil!' exclaimed Waring, taking a little cup from the mantelpiece and turning it round and round as if examining the pattern. 'Not like some girls, who are either killing sweet, or snub you right and left. You are gentle and grave. I used to think I should never have the pluck to ask you to marry me, but—a—you see, when Mrs Newburgh came to grief, I was ashamed of not offering at least to be of use to you.'

'And are you content that I should

accept you as a refuge from the ills of poverty?' asked Mona, looking gravely, calmly at him.

'I am,' said Waring, after a minute's pause, putting down the cup, and speaking more collectedly. 'It's not pleasant, of course, but I have faith in you. If you *promise* to be my wife, you will try to like me, and I'll try to please you with all my soul and with all my strength, as somebody says in the Bible, I think,' added Waring, to enforce his professions —his religious studies were slight, and somewhat mixed. 'And it will go hard if I don't get you to love me, unless—unless,' his large brown eyes grew imploring — 'you care for some other fellow! For God's sake, don't say you love any other fellow! I never fancied you did.'

'I do not indeed.' Her tone carried conviction to her hearer.

'Then—then, Miss Joscelyn, could you make up your mind to marry me? I think you might grow to like me by-and-by, and I need not say I would be delighted to carry out any plan, *any*,' with emphasis, 'that you think would

be best for Mrs Newburgh's comfort ?'

'It is a tremendous question to answer,'
said Mona, hesitating, yet feeling she
must accept him. There was no other
way left, and she was touched by his
unaffected humility. 'Yesterday or the
day before I looked on you as a stranger;
to-day I am to decide if I am to pass
my whole life with you or not. I must
say what sounds unkind, that I do *not*
love you, that if this great misfortune
had not befallen Mrs Newburgh, I should
probably have refused you—so I do not
deserve your love!'

'But I cannot help giving it to you!
And if you *do* make up your mind to
take me, you might just let me forget
that you were driven to it.'

'Yes; I am very ungracious. There
is another circumstance I ought to mention; you may not like to know that
my name is not Joscelyn. My grandmother always called me by my second
baptismal name; I am really Mona Craig.
My father was of very humble origin, I
believe; and Mrs Newburgh never for-

gave my mother for marrying him ; but
I dearly loved him as a little child,
though I have forgotten what he was
like.'

' I don't care what your name is, as
long as you will take mine. *I* am no
great thing as regards family myself. I
have heard something of Mrs Newburgh's
whim before.'

' Is it possible ? '

' I don't fancy that anything is a secret,'
said Waring. ' Perhaps it is not fair to
press you for an answer to-day. But
you see time flies, and I long to be able
to tell Sir Robert Everard that I have
a right to discuss with him what is best
to be done. Don't you fancy that I
would hold back because you refused
me. Whether you say yes or no, I would
ask nothing better than to be of use to
you ; but not being a relation, it would
be awkward for—'

' It would be impossible,' interrupted
Mona, in a low tone ; then pressing her
clasped hands together tightly, she said
with some solemnity,—' Since you believe
I could make you happy—'

'You will be my wife?' interrupted Waring eagerly in his turn.

'I will, Mr Waring, and try to be a good one.' She grew very pale as she spoke.

'You are a great deal too good for me; and as you do not care for any other fellow, perhaps you may end by caring for me.'

There was an awkward pause, then Waring walked over to the writing-table and took up a paper-knife with which he played nervously.

'There are one or two things I should like to tell you, if you do not mind?

'What can he be going to confess?' thought Mona. She however only bent her head in silence.

'I have not been as steady as I ought to be,' resumed Waring, looking down and growing red. 'You see, my brother and myself were brought up by an old bachelor guardian. We had no women in the house, and that made us rather rough. Then I have lost a good bit at cards and races. I'm a little too fond o play, but—now that you are so very

good as to promise me your hand, I
have an object to live for, and I will
never touch a card again, and never lay
anything beyond a pony on a race, and,
and I'll try to be—not unworthy of you.
I will indeed! Now, have I your per-
mission to go and tell Sir Robert
Everard? He is a good fellow, and
we'll settle something about Mrs Newburgh. She ought to get out of town
away from annoyances.'

'Thank you,' returned Mona, touched
by his eagerness to serve her. 'I am
most grateful to you, Mr Waring.'

'Couldn't you manage to call me
Leslie?' he said entreatingly. 'If you
knew how I long to hear my name from
your lips! and to call you Mona. It's not
a happy enough name for you, but I
love it all the same. I can't call you
Mona, if you say Mr Waring.'

'It seems so strange,' murmured
Mona.

'Well, never mind to-day; but I may
go to Sir Robert?'

'You may,' said Mona, with white
lips.'

'Thank you!' cried Waring, his eyes lighting up, his whole face radiant, and so far carried away with joy that he took and kissed her hand, letting it drop directly. 'I suppose I ought to go away now?' he said humbly, 'but I should like to stay. It is almost impossible to believe that you have really promised to marry me, that I may stay and talk to you, and will not have to give up my place to anyone! That fellow Lisle always came and turned me out when we were at Harrowby Chase; but he isn't half bad. Do you know, it was he that advised me to try my chance with you?'

'Did you want advising?' said Mona, in an unsteady voice.

'No, not advising, only heartening up! Tell me—would you like to travel on the Continent? I haven't been much abroad myself. Of course I always go to Paris for the Grand Prix, and to the Baden Races—but you?'

'Everything must depend on my grandmother's condition,' interrupted Mona. 'And, Mr Waring—if you do not think it very rude—I think I must go to her now.'

'You are looking very white,' he said tenderly, 'so I will leave you; but I hope you are not unhappy, and if there is anything you would wish me to do, you will say so?'

Poor Mona longed to cry.

'I only wish you to go away!' she said, pressing her hand to her heart. 'I am a good deal shaken and upset; to-morrow—'

'Oh, yes! I may come to-morrow! And Mona (I may call you Mona, mayn't I?), when you are talking to Mrs Newburgh, just say to her from me that it would be so much better if we —if, that is, if the marriage was to take place soon—quite soon! I should be so much better able to be of use. You'll not think me a bore for insisting on this? but it would really be better, putting my feelings quite out of the question.'

'I shall be guided by what you and Sir Robert and grannie think best,' faltered Mona. 'I am afraid I must go now.'

'When may I come to-morrow?' asked Waring, lingering.

'Oh! at two or three!'

'Well, I see you are tired, and you'll think kindly of me? You know I would do anything for you, *anything!*'

'Oh, yes, I will! And now good-bye.'

Waring caught her hand and looked eagerly at her. For one dread moment her heart fainted within her. Was he going to ask for a kiss? If he had aspired to such a favour, he wisely postponed the demand, and again pressing her long, slight fingers to his lips, he left the room.

Mona ascended the stairs very slowly and deliberately, painfully conscious that she had fully committed herself. It now remained to complete the sacrifice by assuming a cheerful aspect before her grandmother. Then, when she had satisfied her, she might escape to regulate her own thoughts, to face the situation she had accepted.

'Well, Mona?' said Mrs Newburgh, looking eagerly with her pitiful eyes into her grand-daughter's face as she approached, while her thin, tremulous hands grasped the arms of her chair nervously.

'Well, dear granny,' sitting down by her and taking one of her hands in both her own, 'I have heard all Mr Waring had to say, *and* I have promised to marry him.'

Mrs Newburgh did not reply. She pressed Mona's hand, and, leaning back in her chair, the tension of her muscles relaxed, and a peaceful expression stole over her face.

'You have done well, Mona,' she said, after a minute's silence. 'You will yet thank me for urging you to this. Yet I did not *urge;* I only recommended you.'

'That was all. Mr Waring and I have been making our confessions. I told him that I was not in love with him, and that had we not met with such a reverse of fortune, I should probably have refused him; and he told me that he had not been too steady, and was addicted to gambling.'

'You were imprudent, Mona. It is not wise to be too frank with the man you are going to marry. He, no doubt, will overlook everything now; but wait till the first cloud comes between you, and he will remind you that you did not care for him.'

'I think Mr Waring is a man who would forgive anything except deceit; and as I have nothing to hide, I shall try to be absolutely truthful with him.'

'Yes, it is best; but, Mona, be truthful with *me*. Are you quite free from any fancy for—for anyone else?'

'Perfectly free, dear granny,' this very steadily.

'Thank God!' ejaculated Mrs Newburgh. 'You have always been a sensible, cool-headed girl, and I firmly believe you will be a prosperous, happy woman. Your conduct in this matter has repaid me for all I have done.'

'It is very sweet to hear you say so,' said Mona gently.

'Tell me,' resumed Mrs Newburgh, 'is Mr Waring anxious that his marriage should take place soon?'

'He is; he begged me to say so when speaking to you. He left me to see

Sir Robert Everard, and consult with
him.'

'That is well. He is our nearest of
kin in town. Do not oppose this excellent young man's desire for a speedy
union, Mona. " There's many a slip 'twixt
cup and lip." '

'Young!' repeated Mona dreamily.
'He is almost too young for me.'

'Nonsense!' cried Mrs Newburgh,
with something of her former briskness.
'He must be seven or eight years older
than you are. What more would you
want?'

'He seems a kind of overgrown schoolboy — so unfinished and undecided. I
feel quite an old woman of the world
near him.'

'So much the better. The superior
ripeness of your nature will give you influence over him. But I do not think
he is so much a boy as you fancy. I
know he is a favourite among men, and
that always is a good sign.'

And so on for half-an-hour and more.
Mrs Newburgh was quite talkative; she
arranged her grand - daughter's future

household, greatly to her own satisfaction, and settled the amount of pin money she ought to have.

At last Mona was set free to commune with her own heart in her chamber, where she sat very still, reviewing her brief past, and trying to sketch the probable future.

The immediate past was too delightful to be dwelt upon, yet it had been a delusion. She had grown to believe that she was an object of tender interest, of admiration bordering on adoration, to a man of wide experience, of acknowledged taste, and behold, his mode of showing sympathy with her in her sudden eclipse was to pass her on to another. She had been but a moment's amusement to this man, and she —it shocked and frightened her to perceive how dear he had become. No doubt, in her inexperience, she had exaggerated much, and accepted many things as meaning more than he intended. She was too proud to complain of him even to herself; all she cared for was to hide the depth of the impression

he had stamped upon her heart, — to
make him believe that she too had but
amused herself, and that she was quite
ready to seize an advantageous opportunity.
She was not revengeful or resentful, only
ground to the dust of self-abasement, and
ready to adopt any expedient to hide
her gaping, bleeding wounds! Then,
as to the future, was it right or high-
principled to seize upon the honest,
generous affection of Leslie Waring, and
turn it into a shield behind which to hide
her total rout? She thought she could
bear everything, if only *this* ingredient
could be eliminated from the witches'
cauldron of mischief which had been
outpoured on her unoffending head.
He *was* an honest gentleman; she could
have liked him well as a friend or a
brother—but as a husband! The idea
was almost intolerable! How could she
honour and obey a mere boy, to whom
she felt infinitely superior in tact and
knowledge? What support or guidance
could he afford her? But she was
pledged to him; she must not fail him;
she was still more profoundly pledged to

her kind grandmother. Like a Roman who was unable to pay his debts, she could but sell herself into slavery. Not that poor Leslie Waring would make a slave of her; he only asked to enslave himself. How was she to live through the weary interval of her engagement? How could she brace herself to affect an interest in life? And then the recollection of his appealing look at parting made her cheek grow pale and her heart beat. Could she again refuse him the kiss he would certainly ask? — the man she had promised to marry, to love and cherish till death 'did them part.' She shuddered, and turned from the thought, leaving the future—its sufferings, its obligations—to the chapter of accidents, as poor puzzled mortals so often must.

CHAPTER IV.

ON THE BRINK.

ST JOHN LISLE had not, however, come off as scathless as
Mona imagined. He had never
been so hard hit by a girl before.
His taste and ambitions led him to bestow
his devotion generally on married women,
as easier, safer, and more amusing.
Hitherto his love had been from his
life a thing 'exceedingly apart.' Mona's
ordinary reserve, broken by occasional
gleams of enthusiasm and earnestness, interested him, by the constant suggestion
of discoveries yet to make ; while her
style of face and figure were delightful
to his eye. In short, her attraction was
irresistible ; he was angry with himself

for yielding to it as he did—for marriage, even the most brilliant marriage, would not suit his views and plans for years to come. Still it grew more and more delightful to be with Mona, to watch for the slight, reluctantly-granted indications of preference which he from time to time won from her ; nothing ever flattered him so deliciously as the first drooping of her white eyelids over the proud, steady eyes that had for months met his gaze so calmly ; the slight tremble of her hand as it lay in his ; the sweet composure which veiled what *he* perceived from all the world. He was absurdly occupied with this quiet, inexperienced girl, who was so womanly, though so young. She cost him some uncomfortable moments too ; still he never so lost his head as to think seriously of marriage. Years hence, when he had attained a high position, and wanted a dignified, well-regulated home, he might look out for a richly-dowered, highly-connected wife. Now, Mona, though well born, on one side at least, was for all purposes of advancement the merest nobody ; yet what a disturbing influence she exercised on his heart or circulation, or whatever it was that throbbed in his pulses, and prompted him to unpleasant spasms of imprudence! All this irritation had reached its highest pitch during his visit to Harrowby Chase; and so softened was the cool-headed man of the world, that, when the blow fell on Mrs Newburgh, which he knew meant life-long poverty to Mona were she not soon rescued, he really thought how he could best serve her, *after* he had considered how he could soonest disentangle himself from the meshes which he felt were weaving themselves round him in the pleasant, free intercourse of country-house life.

He therefore caught eagerly at Leslie Waring's proposition, and resolved that no illusions about himself should interfere to prevent Mona accepting the deliverance offered to her.

Resolute as he was, both by nature and cultivation, he half-dreaded the interview he had planned so cunningly. He expected tears, agitation, despair, however she might seek to hide their

real source. He even anticipated some
delightful moments. When sympathising
in her distress, and deploring the exi-
gency of his own narrow circumstances,
he might offer consolation in a tender
embrace, and a few—perhaps a good
many—passionate kisses.

Her mode of receiving his communication amazed him. He did not know
what to think. He felt almost sure
that she loved him, and even more sure
that at the present stage of her existence she was unworldly, and remarkably
indifferent to rank and riches. He could
not understand how it was that she fell
in so readily with his suggestion, and
was, in truth, mortified in no small degree,
when he found that the elaborate scheme
of soothing caresses and ingenious rea-
soning he had prepared, was so much
trouble wasted. If she had cared for
him, she could not be so good hum-
ouredly composed,—some stinging words
would have escaped her lips, some indi-
cation of the rage and pain that must
be gnawing her heart would have been
visible.

He was absurdly anxious to see her again—to ascertain if she still kept up the same friendly ease which had baffled him. Meantime he waited in London while his uncle was engaged in arranging with the military big-wigs the details of his new command. It would be much better to go out to India free and unfettered, to know Mona was unable to reproach him. Still, an odd soreness surrounded her image, which was so deeply stamped upon his mind. He was determined to see her again.

A few days after having called in vain at Mrs Newburgh's, Lisle had been breakfasting with General Stafford, and had remained for some time discussing plans. Walking down Piccadilly to his club, he found himself face to face with Sir Robert Everard.

'Ha, Lisle! did not know you were in town!' cried the Baronet.

'And I did not expect to see you at this season, too?'

'I was obliged to come up on account of Mrs Newburgh's business. They won't leave the old woman a rap. First call made yesterday—fifty pounds a share. That will pretty well clear her out. Very foolish to have gone so deep as she did. However, all's well that ends well. Leslie Waring has proposed to Miss Joscelyn, is accepted, and I can tell you, " Haste to the Wedding " is the tune now, ha, ha, ha !—most lucky. Capital fellow, Waring ! going to do the thing handsomely ; but he and the grand-mother are in such a deuce of a hurry that he has decided on a post-nuptial settlement, so I fancy the marriage will come off in a week or so—no grass growing allowed.'

'Very glad to hear it. Miss Joscelyn is far too charming a person to be sub-jected to the revolting ills of poverty. Waring is a lucky fellow to be able to seize what is no doubt a fortunate op-portunity.'

'Ay, the fair lady might have given a different answer had this crash not come. No matter, Mona was always a good, quiet girl,—one of the domesticated sort, that will stick to her house and her man.'

'A somewhat cat-like character,' said Lisle, laughing. 'To me, Miss Joscelyn is an ideal woman.'

'I suspect a little ideal goes a long way with you.'

'Oh! I am a more imaginative person than you think. I must call and offer my congratulations.'

'Well, you had better look in for tea. Mrs Newburgh comes down when the house is shut up, and the lights are lit—then you won't interrupt the billing and cooing, ha, ha, ha! Good-bye.'

'Well-meaning old idiot,' muttered Lisle, as he went on his way with knit brows. ' "The billing and cooing,"—how infernally suggestive. I will just drop in at that particular period, and see if I can interpret the indications aright.'

Lisle was, however, too impatient to calculate time accurately, and Mona was talking with a lady when he was announced. A dark-eyed well-dressed lady, in black cashmere, and bugles with many touches of yellow in tufts of ribbon, and chrysanthemums in her bonnet, enlivening the whole.

Mona had a slight colour, and looked remarkably well. She received Lisle with quiet civility, and immediately introduced him to 'Madame Debrisay.' Lisle bowed low, while he mentally consigned the objectionable third party to the infernal regions. Madame Debrisay looked very keenly at him, and closed her lips with unusual tightness.

Having inquired tenderly for Mrs Newburgh, Lisle said, in a soft tone,—

'I presume, from what Sir Robert Everard told me, I may venture to offer my very sincere congratulations on your approaching marriage with my good friend Leslie.'

'Thank you very much,' returned Mona, with sweet gravity.

There was a pause—mercifully broken by Madame Debrisay, who, with a marked French accent, observed,—

'He is most amiable, the young gentleman, and deserves the good fortune which has befallen him.'

'Those concerned in affairs of this kind are usually considered angels all round,' said Lisle cynically. 'In this case, I only feel inclined to believe in the angelic qualities of one. May I hope to have the pleasure of seeing Mrs Newburgh?'

'She rarely comes down till past three. I will let her know you are here; you were always a favourite of hers.'

Mona rang, and sent a message to Mrs Newburgh to that effect; then Madame Debrisay began to make her adieux.

'I ought not to take up any more of your time, *chérie.*'

'Pray do not go away yet,' cried Mona, with suspicious eagerness.

'She does not want to be alone with me,' thought Lisle. 'Why does not that horrid woman go? She must know she is in the way.'

'Indeed, dear, I have one or two things to do before I go home, for next week I shall be in harness again; but I will be with you by ten o'clock to-morrow. Nothing like the early hours for shopping; and make my compliments to—'

'Mr Waring,' announced Wehner, and Waring entered, with an eager, not to say anxious, expression, as if not too certain how he would be received.

Madame Debrisay, who was near the door, made him a respectful courtesy, and he greeted her first.

'How do you do, madame? Not going, I hope, because I have come in.'

Here he paused, for Mona turned to him with a kind, welcoming smile, so much the sweetest she had ever bestowed on him, that he grew positively radiant, and evidently forgot there was anyone else present. Lisle took it all in, and gazed with surprise and admiration at Mona. If this was acting, it was a marvellous imitation of nature; if not, what a weather-cock this grave, gently-dignified young creature must be!

'I think grannie would like to see you,' said Mona, following Madame Debrisay. 'Excuse me for a moment,' looking back to her visitors. 'Oh! why do you go, Deb? I dread these *tête-à-tête* interviews.'

'But Captain Lisle is a third, dear.'

'Oh, he will go away directly.'

'Ah! my child, don't give way to these

whims. Sure you'll have to pass your whole life *tête-à-tête* with him ; and he is good—real, downright good. Make much of him. Go back now, and I'll not fail to be with you to-morrow at ten.'

At the other side of the door, Lisle was congratulating Waring in the frankest and most cordial manner.

' I consider a great deal is due to me for spiriting you up, my dear fellow. Nothing venture, nothing have—so you won a prize any man might be proud of.'

' Haven't I though ! I went to the right man for advice. I say, Lisle, won't you be my best man ? '

' I am afraid I'll be half way to India when the happy event comes off.'

' Oh ! we are going ahead at a great rate. We—or I should say I—hope to fix it for Tuesday fortnight.'

' Sharp work, eh ? '

Here Mona returned.

' I do not think my grandmother will come down just yet, Captain Lisle.'

' Sorry I shall not have the pleasure of seeing her. I shall be going to India in about six weeks, and I have to go to Paris to see my sister, etc., etc.' The talk flowed on in ordinary channels for a few minutes, and then Lisle rose to take leave. 'Should I not see you again as Miss Joscelyn,' he said, as he pressed her hand, 'you will remember that you have my warmest good wishes for your happiness. I shall pay my respects to Mrs Newburgh on my return to London; so goodbye.'

Mona flushed, and paled quickly.

'And I wish you all possible success; so goodbye,' she said slowly.

Waring, in his gratitude, went with him downstairs, and bid him an effusive farewell at the hall door, returning in high glee to Mona, who was putting some more coal on the fire.

'Oh, let me do that. Why do you trouble? Isn't the room hot enough?'

'Grannie will be down soon, and she never finds it warm.'

'Not just yet, I hope. Somehow or other I never seem to get a moment alone with you, Mona. I was glad to see the back of Lisle, though he is a capital fellow. I don't know that I like any fellow better; but I was dying to tell you how happy you made me just now when I came in; you really looked as if you were glad to see me. If I thought you were going to be fond of me, even half as fond of me as I am of you, why, I should be almost off my head with joy.'

'You are too good to me,' she returned sadly, for his words and tone touched her.

'I know,' he went on, 'that you do not care much for me now, but I begin to hope you will. Give me your hand: how long and slender it is! You could not do much with it, Mona. Why do you draw it away? Hallo! your ring has slipped off! I don't like that. Let me put it on again. Now, give me a kiss for luck; you have never given me but one kiss, and I have dreamed of it ever since—just one more, Mona!'

And Mona—shocked at her own reluctance, ashamed of her own coldness towards the man who had given her his whole heart—compelled herself to turn her pale, fair face to him.

Clasping her hand in both his own, Waring bent down and pressed his lips lingeringly on hers. He scarcely dared to embrace her. His frame trembled; his eyes were moist.

'Say Leslie, I will try to love you,' he whispered.

'I will try—I will indeed, Leslie,' she repeated. 'I have been so uneasy and unhappy about poor grannie; and I never thought of marrying so soon; and altogether I have been shaken and nervous —so you must forgive me if I seem stupid.'

'Stupid! You stupid! What an idea!'

Meanwhile Lisle walked down the street in anything but pleasant self-commune.

'I certainly troubled myself unnecessarily about my charming young friend. She has thrown me over easily enough; she must think me a soft idiot to have troubled myself advising or directing her. Were I to remain in town, I might teach Mrs Leslie Waring that I was no foolish stripling, to be tossed aside with indifference and impunity when fate offered her fairer fortune! She knows that it cost me a bad quarter of an hour to give her up for her own good. Who can calculate on the strange variations of feminine nature?'

So argued Lisle, with the degree of logic usual in men whose vanity has been wounded. He was quite willing that Mona should be taken out of his way, but he should have liked to see her weeping—broken-hearted at the loss of his fascinating self. Yet, although horribly irritated, he probably never longed more passionately to be in Waring's place — always provided the engagement, marriage, what you will, was not to be permanent.

Both Mrs Newburgh and Sir Robert Everard were very urgent that the wedding should take place as soon as possible. Waring, though eager on this point, was too fearful of incurring Mona's displeasure to express himself as warmly as he felt. It was always, ' What would *you* like, Mona?' ' Whatever you choose, dear!' This excessive deference to her wishes almost wearied

her. In her present mood she did not
care to think or decide about anything.
Nor did she oppose the wishes of her
relatives. She had fully committed herself; perhaps the sooner the question of
her future was fixed beyond recall, the
sooner she would throw off the disturbing
pain which the possibility of escape
created, so long as she was still unmarried. Moreover, she hated to receive
the presents with which Leslie Waring
tried to overwhelm her. It cost her an
effort to thank him, and still another
to explain that it would be more pleasing
to her to take them from her husband's
hands.

She was completely cured of her love for
the man St John Lisle had proved himself to be; but both heart and fancy
clung still to the being her imagination
had depicted. It was too soon to endure
the thought of another lover. Had
time been granted her for the effer-
vescence of her spirit to subside—for
her cruel wounds to heal, she might
have been won to regard Waring with
kindly affection; as it was, her whole

nature revolted from being forcibly plunged into the tremendous intimacy of married life with a stranger.

This period of engagement was by no means as blissful as Waring anticipated. Mona, though gentle and complaisant, was cold—colder than she knew — and Waring was sometimes tempted to ask her if the sacrifice to which she had consented was too cruel. Then some strain of compassion would steal over her heart, and thrill her voice or soften her eyes, and the poor boy— for he was but a boy, in spite of his years—would be lifted to the seventh heaven of joyous anticipation. He had the most unbounded faith in Mona, and he had her assurance that she did not love anyone. His devotion, then, must win her. How formidable the rivalry of that first unfulfilled dream of love was, he could not know. Would he learn it hereafter ?

' Well, Mrs Newburgh,' said Sir Robert Everard, who had again come up to town on his relative's account, ' I am very glad that everything is so satisfactorily settled. I must say Mona is a capital, sensible girl, and makes no fuss or bother about clothes. Waring's idea of doing their shopping together in Paris is first-rate. He will sign a will in his wife's favour as soon as they return from church; and meantime the post-nuptial settlement is being prepared. Really, Waring is most generous. What are you going to do?'

'I am going to stay on here. I think my poor house is tolerably safe for a few months. Mr Waring talks of renting a place in some good hunting county —indeed, I think he is in treaty for one— and he has very courteously invited me to make my home with him. For the present, I have accepted. So old a woman as I have become in the last month, cannot be much in the way, and probably I shall not trouble them long. Though infinitely relieved, and thankful that Mona is provided for so happily, I do not gather strength. These terrible. palpitations and faintness seem to sap my life; but I am not uneasy; my work is done—quite done!'

'Come, come! I hope to drink your health on your eightieth birthday, my dear lady! we must have no doleful ideas of that kind. So the happy day is fixed for the first. Lady Mary and the girls will come up the day before, and that will be all the company.'

'Yes, all! It is very good of you to curtail your visit to the moors on our account.'

'"Blood is thicker than water"' returned Sir Robert, and after a little further cheerful talk and gossip, which did not seem to interest Mrs Newburgh as much as it used, the Baronet took leave.

'Your mistress does not pick up as fast as we could wish,' he said to Wehner, who helped him on with his overcoat in the hall.

'No, Sir Robert. She is not strong; she is very weak—weaker each day. It grieves me to the heart.'

'Ay! she is a good mistress. Now you will be sent adrift before long, I am afraid.'

'Yes, sir.'

'Well, I'll bear you in mind.'

'Thank you, Sir Robert.'

This conversation had taken place when Mona was engaged in some unavoidable shopping with Madame Debrisay. Having done all they could before the light failed them, Mona begged to be allowed to take tea with her friend.

'You know I have never seen your new rooms, Deb.'

'Then come, and welcome. We will go into Whiteley's and get some tea-cakes. Tea-cakes are, to my mind—or maybe I ought to say to my palate—the *ne plus ultra* of goody! I suppose Mrs Newburgh will not mind your being late?'

'No ; she knows I am with you ; besides, Sir Robert Everard is to be in town to-day, and she likes to have his visits all to herself. They have many memories in common,—though he is much younger.'

'And Mr Waring?'

'He has gone down to Leicestershire to look at a place that is to be let there.'

'Well, well, you are the lucky girl, Mona!'

'I suppose so.'

They drove on in silence to the

Universal Provider's, and thence walked
to Madame Debrisay's new quarters.

'How nice and quiet it is here!' cried
Mona, taking off her hat and drawing a
chair to the fire, which Madame Debrisay stirred and incited to burning, with
some sticks drawn from a cupboard beside the fireplace. 'Quite a good-sized
room too; but, Deb dear, it might be
tidier!'

'So it might; but, *ma belle*, I have
no time; and what does the poor slave
of a girl know of tidiness? besides, if
she tried her hand, I'd never find my
bits of things.'

Mona's remark was not uncalled for.
The apartment was sadly littered. A cottage piano had an old Indian shawl arranged as a drapery at the back, one
side of which was unfastened; piles of
music lay on it, and on a broken-backed
chair; a heap of crumpled newspapers
on another; a small round table was
crowded with plants, many of them withered; and sundry garments in process of
mending or making were loosely rolled
together on the ottoman. This, and a

generally undusted aspect, did not improve the appearance of the room. It was on the ground floor, and looked out on a general garden, which at that season was anything but cheerful.

'I have an elegant bedroom to the front,' resumed Madame Debrisay. 'Come and look at it.' Passing a glass door at the top of the kitchen stair, she opened it, and called,—'Amelia, bring up the tea kettle; I'll boil it myself.' 'It's a great convenience being able to cry down for what you want. Now, there's my bedroom. I am afraid it is not in much better order than the other.'

'I can't say that it is, Deb, but it is nearly as large as the other. I wonder you do not make this your salon. The lookout is more cheerful.'

'I am not much in by daylight. Then you see the other room has a fine white marble chimney-piece. It was intended for the drawing-room. These houses used to be expensive, but they have come down like myself. Come along, and I'll make the tea.'

'I think,' said Mona presently, as she slowly stirred her cup, 'it would be nice to do some of the housework oneself.'

'I suspect a little of it would go a long way with you. It's little work you'll have to do. There's an easy life before—'

' " To sit on a cushion and sew up a seam, and eat ripe strawberries, sugar, and cream" all day long, is not exactly my idea of a blissful existence,' said Mona.

'Now, my darling, I am going to give you a good scolding. You are looking pale and thin, and your eyes are as solemn as if you were going to a funeral. Is that the way to treat the dear, generous, elegant young man who's ready to worship the ground you walk on? What is it you want? I did not think you were the sort of girl who would cry for the moon.'

'Nor am I,' returned Mona thoughtfully. 'I know, Deb, that Mr Waring is too good for me—'

'I don't say that. No one on earth

is too good for you, in my mind,' interrupted Madame Debrisay.

'But—let me confess myself to you. I would give *anything*—anything not to be obliged to marry him. It is foolish, unreasonable. I know it is. Yet I have such a vision of weariness before me. I know I shall be sick to death of being with him. I never know what to say to him.'

'I warrant he knows what to say to *you !*' cried Madame.

'No! indeed he does not! He can only tell me I am perfection, and that he adores me.'

'It's a style of conversation few young ladies would object to.'

'Well, I do. Yet I am so sorry for him. Poor fellow, he *does* love me.'

'Ah! well you see some of that will rub off when he is married. A lover is one thing, and husband is quite another. Then oughtened you to be glad to make a human being happy ?'

'Shall I make him happy ? I doubt it. Oh, Deb, Deb! I would give the world for freedom and work. I

am tired of pleasure and an aimless
existence.'

'*Dieu des Dieux!* Does that mean
you are in love with some penniless
scamp?'

'No, dear. At least I am guiltless
of marrying one man while my heart
aches for another.'

'Then there is something underneath
I do not understand. If you don't
care for anyone else, all will come
right. You talk to me a year hence,
and you'll have a different story to tell.
Now, I'll not speak another word on
the subject. I hate talking of what I
don't understand. Take another cup, my
angel.'

For all reply, Mona burst into tears,
not a violent outburst, but a quietly
bitter flow, with deep suppressed sobs.

'My dear child! what's all this
about?' cried Madame Debrisay, with
unfeigned concern. 'What's troubling
you? Sure, you used to tell me all
your sorrows when you used to come
to me for your music lesson in Paris.
Tell me now.'

'I really have nothing to tell,' said Mona, struggling with her tears. 'It is just a nervous attack,—a "crise," as you used to call it. I have felt tearful and unstrung ever since I was startled by grannie's telegram at Harrowby Chase, and I have been on the stretch ever since. I suppose it sounds very foolish, Deb, but I wish I could come and live with you, and help you in some way, rather than—'

'Oh! hush—hush—my darling. You are meant for better things. There's no one would be so welcome as yourself; but there is a different life before you.'

'Should I really be welcome to you, Deb, suppose everyone turned from me?'

'Hoot toot! Yes, of course. Come —I must not let you talk any more nonsense. I'll make the girl call a cab, and take you straight away home.'

CHAPTER V.

THE GREAT KING.

IME flew swiftly. A red frosty
sun, rose on the morning before
Mona was to be changed into
Mrs Leslie Waring.

She had been persuaded to sleep in
her own room again, as Mrs Newburgh
seemed so much better, and quite re-
conciled to a nice new maid—sent her
from the country by Lady Mary
Everard.

'How is my grandmother?' was Mona's
first question, when this functionary
brought her hot water.

'Nicely, miss; she was fast asleep when
I left the room.'

'I will ring as soon as I am dressed.
Did you speak to Mrs Newburgh?'

'No, miss; she looked so still and
quiet, I thought it best not to disturb
her.

'Perhaps you are right! I will come
directly.'

Mrs Newburgh's eyes were open when
her grand-daughter approached, she
smiled, kindly and faintly. When Mona
asked her if she would like to get up,
she smiled a peculiar dreamy kind of
smile, and murmured in a muffled
voice,—

'Yes, dear, of course I should.'

Mona therefore put her arm under
her shoulders to help her in rising, which
was always a little difficult.

'Thank you, my love,' she said, in
the same indistinct way, smiling as she
spoke, and sitting on the side of the
bed; her feet did not at first touch the
floor.

Assisted by Mona, she put them down
resolutely, but fell back immediately,
silent and motionless.

It took all Mona's strength to keep

her inert form from slipping off the
bed, while she stretched her hand to the
bell-rope which hung beside it. The new
lady's-maid came running at the summons.

'Help me to lay her down!' whispered
Mona.

She felt terrified; this was somehow
different from Mrs Newburgh's usual
fainting fits.

The maid assisted to place her in bed.
She was rigid, and very heavy.

'Fan her, Ellen,' said Mona, as she
turned away to get some restorative.

'Lord bless us, ma'am!' exclaimed the
woman, in an awe-struck tone; 'I do
believe she is gone!'

'Impossible!' cried Mona, rushing to
her side. 'Why she has only just been
speaking to me. She often faints; send
for the doctor.'

'Ah! no doctor will do her any good,
poor lady; her heart is quite still,' laying
her hand on it, 'and her eyes,—just look
at them, miss—open and glassy.'

Mona took one of the helpless hands
in both her own : the touch chilled her.

'I cannot believe it. Try and give

her this,' hastily measuring out the prescribed quantity of medicine.

Ellen shook her head — and obeyed. It was in vain. Wehner was despatched for the doctor, but before he came— Mona's hopes were over. Her grandmother, her one real friend was dead. She could not doubt what that grey pallor, the deadly stillness, the stiffened form meant—still she could not realise that she should never hear her speak, never turn to her for guidance, never attend to her little wants again.

The doctor came quickly, and at once declared that life was quite extinct,—that he had always anticipated a sudden death for his patient. Her heart was weak, and so much emotion as had tried her of late, had rendered all exertion, all agitation, dangerous ; and probably the effort to rise, and stand up, was the final feather which broke the strained cord of life.

There was no more to be done! What desolation there is in that sentence. All the warmth of the most glowing love, all the force of the strongest will, are

powerless to roll away the stone from
the sepulchre of our hopes, once death
has placed it there!

It seemed to poor dazed Mona that
Sir Robert and Lady Mary Everard
appeared as if by magic. What a solace
it was to throw herself into kind Lady
Mary's arms, and tell her brokenly how
deeply she mourned the thoughtful—if
tyrannical protectress, to whom misfortune had linked her so closely.

'Well, dear, you may rest assured that
the near prospect of your marriage
soothed and brightened her last hours;
and it is a great comfort to know she
was in a happy frame of mind. Sir
Robert has sent round to Mr Waring.
He will be here immediately, no doubt,
and will be your best support.'

'Oh! no, no! *You* are best. You
knew poor dear grannie so well, and she
was *so* fond of you.'

'Dear old lady! Of course, at such
a painful crisis, old friends count for a
great deal. I think, dear, you must come
back with me to Charles Street. I cannot leave you here alone.'

'No, Lady Mary, I will not leave the
house while poor grannie lies helpless
here.   I feel bound to keep by her to
the last.'

A message from Sir Robert brought
Waring as fast as a well-paid driver could
urge his horse.   He was quite sorry for
the old lady, who had always treated him
with kindly deference.   He was deeply
sympathetic with his peerless Mona, *but*
he was principally put out because he
knew that in commonest decency his
marriage must be delayed.   Mona was
not in the drawing-room when he reached
it, and he was somewhat discomfited
when Lady Mary came and explained
that Mona was too much overcome to
see him,—that she was in her own room.

'But she *will* see me presently, will
she not?' he asked appealingly.   'I
thought it might be a comfort to her
to talk to me.'

'No doubt it will be.   At this moment
she is terribly upset.'

It was not till considerably later—after
Waring and Sir Robert had arranged
the details of the funeral, and all that

appertained to it — that Mona was induced to see her affianced husband.

Lady Mary thought it was kindest to leave them alone, for which poor Waring thanked her from the depths of his heart, but the interview was productive of little pleasure to him.

Mona was ready enough to speak of her sorrow. She was gently grateful for his sympathy, but she would not sit beside him, her head on his shoulder, and his arm round her, nor did she permit a course of consolation compounded of whispers, kisses, and assurances that the whisperer would be brother and sister and grandmother and everything to her. She was so dazed and overwhelmed that Waring was gravely uneasy about her, and it was an immense relief to him to know that Madame Debrisay (who had heard of the sad event in some occult manner) was in the house, and would spend the night with her favourite pupil.

· · · · · · · ·

Established custom governs all things —the deepest grief — the wildest joy.

The dreary days—which lingered yet went so swiftly—sped on, and poor Mrs Newburgh was laid in her grave. Her will, leaving all she possessed to Mona, was duly read—her few jewels and personalities packed up. The former went with Mona to Harrowby Chase. Her books, her favourite chair, a few pieces of plate and china, were taken charge of by Madame Debrisay, and the Green Street house, pending the action of the liquidators, was to be let.

Mona took cold on her journey, and for a fortnight was very unwell — so feverish, in fact, as to wander in her speech, and to cause her kind hosts a good deal of anxiety. Her nerves had been greatly shaken; she was weaker and more depressed than could have been anticipated. She was very averse to speak, and used to sit brooding for hours.

She was utterly lonely. She had no near relative. The Everards were more closely allied by friendship than by blood to Mrs Newburgh. She had heard of many other cousins in her grandmother's lifetime, but she felt they did not count. Of Lord Sunderline, her nearest of kin, she knew but very little, nor was that little attractive.

Pondering these things, she grew affrighted at the stern aspect of the world she was going to face, for, as she collected her faculties and studied her circumstances, she grew more and more averse to fulfil her engagement with Leslie Waring. The great motive was gone, and an irresistible longing for freedom, however poverty stricken, seized her. The idea of so close a union with a mere good-natured sportsman, who in no way touched her imagination, whose offensive affection wearied her, whose personal appearance was unpleasant to her eye, became infinitely repugnant as she dwelt upon it. It was hardly fair to him either to let him plunge into the irrevocable in ignorance of her aversion. Better let him bear a temporary pang now, than incur the misery long drawn out of an ill-assorted, unsympathetic marriage.

Her resolution to break with him grew

rapidly stronger almost before she was aware she had formed it. Then she began to see that she was enjoying Lady Mary's kind hospitality under false pretences. She did not for a moment doubt that her refusal to marry Waring would bring down, if not a storm of wrath—for Lady Mary and her family were far too well - bred to be violently angry—but an iceberg of disapprobation. She must remove herself from the shelter of their roof before she struck the blow that would give poor Waring so much temporary pain. (She felt sure it would be but temporary.) And where could she go? There was no one but her faithful Madame Debrisay on whom she could count, and even she would be very very angry. Still her purpose grew clearer and firmer as her nervous system began to recover the shock it had sustained.

'Pray, dear, did poor Mrs Newburgh leave any ready money?' asked Lady Mary, coming into her husband's dressing-room, where he was occupied with his toilette, after a sharp and satisfactory run with the Daleshire hounds.

'Yes; a few hundreds, which she put in my hands to meet immediate expenses. Why do you ask?'

'Oh, Mona told me to ask you! She came downstairs to luncheon to-day, looking very white and miserable, poor child; she seems restless, and anxious to go out of the way of our Christmas gathering. She proposes to spend a short time with Madame Debrisay—a very respectable person; she gave Evelyn music lessons, and—'

'Why the deuce doesn't she marry Waring straight off, and go away with him? that's the sort of change that would set her up.'

'Well, you see, she feels it would be indecently soon after her grandmother's death.'

'Pooh! nonsense! Why, nothing would please the old lady so much, even if she were in heaven, as to know the knot was absolutely tied! You make her hear reason. Let us send for Waring; she has her wedding-gown, and we will marry them next week.'

'I wish I could,' ejaculated Lady Mary.

'By the way, what has become of Waring?'

'He has gone to see his old guardian about some business; to pass away the time, I fancy, till Mona is well enough to see him. He was quite distracted about her at first, poor fellow. I really do not think she is half as grateful to him as she ought to be.'

'No; I daresay not—it would be unfeminine! But he ought not to put up with such rubbish. Who is this woman she wants to go to?'

'I told you, my dear. She is a professor of music, well known to us all.'

'Well, you ought to ascertain what Waring thinks about it—he has a right to be consulted.'

'I do not think he would object. Then he could stay in London and see her every day; whereas a man so much in love is rather a nuisance in a house.'

'Oh, manage it your own way! Marry them out of hand if you can. Perhaps it might be as well to let her go ; for I want a really nice party to meet Lord Finistoun, who is a capital fellow, and it is his first visit here. Mind you, I don't think Mona is treating Waring well ; you ought to influence her.'

'That is not so easily done. She has some of the Newburgh blood, you know, and thinks she knows her own mind.'

' Bah ! I thought better of Mona.'

The jovial country gentleman was too much occupied with his pleasures and affairs to trouble about feminine crotchets —all that was Lady Mary's work.

Meantime, Mona had not been idle. She wrote to her ' dear Deb,' begging leave to visit her, as she felt herself an impediment to the party Lady Mary wished to assemble, and also because she had more to say than she could write.

This brought a speedy, rapturous reply.

Then Mona applied herself to compose, re-write, and copy her difficult letter to Leslie Waring.

It was even a worse task than she

anticipated. All her selfish longing for deliverance was for the moment swallowed up in sorrow for the pain she was about to inflict. Nothing kept her steady to her purpose so much as her conviction that she was doing right,— that she was delivering Leslie as well as herself. She was more than one day over her task ; for Evelyn Everard, an exceedingly girlish girl, who had taken a violent fancy to her, was constantly running into her room with her work, or book, or for the avowed intention of 'enlivening' her.

It was accomplished at last, however ; but Mona waited to post it till she was safe in town, even though she left two of Waring's epistles unanswered. Indeed, her replies had always been few and scanty—so much so, that even he had become restless and dissatisfied. He hoped, however, that a personal interview would put all matters right. Mona had had so severe a shock in the sudden death of her grandmother in her very arms, that she must be shown all patience and consideration.

It was with a nervous sense of guilt, of being a deceiver, that Mona took leave of Lady Mary and her daughters. She took advantage of the Vicar's wife's company, as she was going to town for a rare visit, and she thus avoided the cost and worry of having a smart lady's-maid sent with her.

It was a grey blustering afternoon when she reached St Pancras, and found Madame Debrisay waiting for her.

'My dear, you *do* look bad! Come, get into the cab. I will find your things.'

'I have only this small portmanteau and bonnet-box for the present.'

'That's right. I am sure you are not fit to be out in such weather, get in ; dear.'

'I must post this letter first,' said Mona, her lips quivering.

'Very well. Give it to me. Oh, yes ; quite right,' glancing at the address. 'You must keep him informed of your whereabouts. It's hard times for him, poor fellow, all this delay.' The long drive to Westbourne Villas passed almost in silence on Mona's side. To Madame Debrisay silence was abhorrent, and she poured out much information respecting the changes she had made in her dwelling—the additional pupils promised her next month. 'I am glad I have the rest of this one comparatively free. I can give a little time to you, my dear child. And here we are, thank God! You will be the better of a cup of tea.'

Mona was, indeed, thankful to have, so far, accomplished her purpose as to be under the roof of her only sympathetic friend; but her heart fainted within her at the thought of the confession she had to make. If Madame Debrisay refused to harbour her, what was she to do? Meantime that busy woman flitted to and fro. She stirred the already glowing fire, made the kettle boil up, infused the tea, and cut brown bread and butter with immense energy, while Mona—having put aside her bonnet and cloak—lay back in a comfortable little basket-chair — indescribable despondency expressed in every line of her slight form—her hands clasped and motionless.

'There now,' said madame, placing a small table with a cup of tea and plate of bread and butter beside her young guest, 'take that, and get warmed. Then say your say, for I can see your heart is full. It's like a ghost you are —an uneasy ghost, dear, that hasn't contrived to deliver its message.'

'I have no doubt of it,' returned Mona, with a faint smile. 'You describe what I feel myself to be, exactly.'

Madame Debrisay looked at her with kind, compassionating eyes, and stirred her own tea reflectively—remaining silent for an unusual length of time.

'Now,' she said, when the refection was finished—having rapidly packed up the cups and saucers, and popped (no other word conveys the action) the tray outside — 'now, come, open your heart to me, dear, for I know you are in trouble.'

'I am indeed,' returned Mona, in a voice that faltered and shook in a way far more touching than the most violent burst of tears. 'I have determined to break off my engagement!'

'And you within a day of being his wife, if your dear sainted grandmother hadn't been swept away in a minute! No, I won't listen to you. It's mad, and bad, and not like yourself at all! What will Sir Robert say, and — and Lady Mary? Who'd have thought you'd be so cruel and false? I must say it, dear! Indeed, I knew there was misfortune coming, since I had your note. And something told me you wouldn't marry him. Ah! my poor Waring! you deserved better at her hands!'

'I knew you would be angry,' said Mona sadly, 'but I cannot help it. I cannot marry him, or anyone. Life is too hard!'

'Ah! then do you think you'll make it softer by keeping single? I know better. Life is cruel to a single woman that's poor, and pretty, and delicately reared, as you are. How do you mean to live? What can you do to earn a crust?'

'Not much, certainly; but I have the will, and I am persevering; and don't

speak so cruelly, Deb, for I feel heart-
broken.'

'God forgive me,' said madame solemnly. 'He knows I would share my
last loaf with you, and will too; but I
am angry with you, my darling. You
are flying in the face of Providence,
and driving an excellent young man to
an early grave.'

'I do not think that, Deb. Nay,
I suppose in a month or two he will
be in love with someone else. I do
not think he is the sort of man who
will destroy himself for an ideal.'

'Tell me the truth, Mona, my dear child.
Are you in love with another, — some
poor creature you can't marry?'

'No; in truth I am not. There is
not a man on the face of the earth at
this moment I would willingly marry.'

'I believe you, for I never knew you
speak falsely yet; but there is something
under it all I can't make out. I always
thought there was. Maybe you will tell
me one day. Now, listen to me. If
you ever cared for your dear, good,
generous grandmother, don't be in a

hurry; just say your prayers, and *think*.
Believe me, it's awfully hard to pick up
a living, especially when you haven't
anyone to take you by the hand. And
you have turned everyone against ye, or
you will. Don't quarrel with the poor
young fellow that has given you his
whole heart. Take a day or two to
think what you're doing.'

'I have done it, Deb,' stretching out
her hand, and laying it on her friend's
plump arm. 'You posted *the* letter to
him yourself, just now.'

'Ah! that was base of you—base, to
take my hand to deal the blow. I'll
never forgive you, never!'

'Yes, you will—you must,' rising and
kneeling beside her, while she clasped her
arms round her waist. 'I have no one in
the world to turn to but you, Deb, and I
cannot marry this man—I cannot indeed.'

'And you have written to him? Then
he will never rest satisfied without seeing you; and when he comes, in the name
of God, let him persuade you.'

'I cannot promise *that*, Deb, dear. I
will not see him if I can help it; but if

he insists, why, I will. He has a right to so much, and I cannot refuse.'

'Oh! that is something. No, don't refuse; you let him persuade you when he does find. I'll be bound when he opens his lips and tells you how he has trusted to your word, he will bring you round. Promise me you will hear him.'

'I will,' said Mona gently; 'and if he insists on keeping me to my word, I will keep it; but—but after reading my letter, I do not think he will.'

'Don't be too sure of that. Now tell me, have you told Lady Mary?'

'Not yet. I thought I would wait till I had his answer.'

'That's right. He'll come and speak his answer himself, or I am much mistaken, and—well, we'll wait and see what it will be.'

'He will not hold me to my word?'

'I am not so sure. Anyway, I'll talk no more to you about him this day. You are just tired and done for. We'll leave the matter to Heaven; and you must rest. Do you remember what you said in your unlucky letter?'

'Yes. I told him I was driven by my grandmother's position to accept him ; that I was heartily ashamed of having misled him ; that I felt it was only just to tell him that I did not, and could not, love him as a wife ought to love ; that I deeply deplored the pain I gave him, and humbly begged his forgiveness ; that I thanked him for his goodness, and prayed that he would forget me, and soon be happy with someone more worthy than myself.'

'Ah ! I know—the usual sort of thing. It would serve you right if he never replied. Ah, Mona, Mona ! this is the biggest mistake ever you made. Still, I'll not turn my back on you, my poor child, and maybe — maybe your luck won't leave you yet.'

CHAPTER VI.

THE TUG OF WAR.

THE change from the luxurious elegance of the 'Chase' to Madame Debrisay's London lodgings, was about as great as can be imagined.

Yet the house was not mean. The 'widow woman' who owned it had a certain refinement. Instead of the usual extremely unlaced and unkempt 'slavey,' she had an elderly servant of neat and imposing aspect, who had been with her for years, and who was rather a terror to Madame Debrisay.

The lodger who occupied the upper floor was a steady elderly city clerk, of remarkable punctuality and precision.

Still the tone of the homely dwelling was new to Mona, who had been accustomed to the aristocratic, if narrow, nicety of her grandmother's house, or the distinction of her relatives' establishments.

The only members of the family who had accepted Mrs Newburgh's granddaughter frankly and cordially, were Sir Robert and Lady Mary Everard. The rest looked on her as an interloper, an offshot tainted by an admixture of blood that was anything but blue. Of this she was but dimly conscious. While under her grandmother's wing, she had been received with decent civility; now, she felt keenly that she was about to alienate the only real friends she possessed —to sink from the level of the Newburgh traditions to that of struggling, almost adventurous, nobodies. Yet she did not regret the desperate step she had taken. Why, at her age, should she link herself for a long life to a thraldom that would irk her soul? Youth demands so much. It takes the friction of a life-time to teach moderation and the wisdom of compromise.

To Mona, the notion of temperate liking, instead of devotion to an ideal hero, and the importunate adoration of a man whom she considered common-place and dull, was intolerable. Above all, she was so disenchanted with life, and love, and dreams of perfection, by St John Lisle's conduct, that she fancied it was impossible the scattered fragments of imagination's shining temple could ever be reformed — not knowing the marvellous recuperative powers of time and nature.

Fatigue made her sleep so profoundly, that it took some moments of waking consciousness before she recognised where she was. The sound of someone moving reminded her that she was sharing Madame Debrisay's room, and presently that lady came out fully dressed from behind a large Japanese screen, which converted one corner into a dressing closet.

'And how did you sleep, dear ? '

'Oh, well ; too well ! ' exclaimed Mona.

'Well, stay where you are. I'll bring you a cup of coffee and a bit of toast, for I have a long, busy day before me. I go to Mrs Ardell's grand establishment first, over at Kensington. I am there for four mortal hours, then I get a bit of food ; and give two private lessons in the same neighbourhood, so I am obliged to leave you nearly all day. But business is business.'

' Of course it is ; do not mind me !'

' My good landlady will give you something to eat at her dinner time, and we will have a cosy tea together when I come in.'

' Thank you, Deb.'

'You see I have taken your advice, and changed my rooms. I was just ready in time for you, my lamb ; the front room *is* better for a sitting-room.'

She hurried away, and returned sooner than Mona could have expected, with a fragrant cup of *café au lait* and a slice of buttered toast.

Once more she put in her head with a cheerful—

' I'm off now, make yourself comfortable, dear ; there are some books and a lot of *Family Heralds* in the next room ;

there are splendid stories in them, they
make your hair stand on end, and forget
the time. Take the hand-bell if you
want anything—none of the other bells
will ring. Good-bye, dear.'

Mona dressed slowly, and went into
the sitting-room. It was a stormy, wet
day. The rain beat against the one large
bow window which lighted it, and which
looked over a small square of grass, with
a flower-bed in the middle, and a couple
of trees next the railings, that divided
it from the street. It was a fairly well-
kept front garden, but at the present
time, being strewn with dead leaves, and
sodden with rain, it was not a cheerful
prospect. The fire had been hastily
loaded with coal, and had succumbed to
the load. The table-cover was crooked;
a very irregular pile of newspapers,
Heralds, programmes of concerts, over-
flowed an occasional table; but the
furniture was good and in good order,
though extremely mixed as to style and
pattern ; some of it, in fact, was Madame
Debrisay's, and some her landlady's.

The hand-bell evoked a tall, hard-

featured woman, with thick grizzled hair,
a spotless cap, and a dark print dress.

'The fire's gone out?' she repeated, in
a high-pitched tone. 'I daresay madame
thinks coals 'll light of theirselves; she
just pitches them on, whether there is
a spark alive or not. I'll fetch a few
sticks, miss.'

The fire burning, the hearth swept, and
a few tidying touches bestowed on the
room, made a vast improvement.

Mona threw herself into an arm-chair,
and tried to think what was best to do.
What pressed most upon her mind was
the painful necessity of communicating
with Lady Mary. She ought not to be
left in ignorance of her intentions, but
would it not be well to hear first what
Leslie Waring would say. Yes, she would
wait.

The previous evening she had posted
a few lines to the Chase, announcing her
safe arrival, she might therefore post-
pone her next letter for twenty-four
hours.

By this time, her refusal to ratify her
engagement had been read by her lover

and she quivered at the idea of the pain and mortification she had inflicted. He would be awfully angry. Indeed, she hoped he would. It might help him to throw off his grief. He would write severely : she dreaded his letter — but surely he would be too bitterly offended to come in person to reproach her ; that possibility was unspeakably terrible.

The dreary hours went slowly by— slowly, yet fast. She could not form any conception of what her future might be. Her powers of imagination, of con- jecture, paused, paralysed, before the bristling difficulties of the present.

She could hardly expect a letter from Waring till the next day. He was staying—not very far away, in Hamp- shire — with the gentleman who had been his guardian, and for whom he had a great regard. This man was— Mona felt, rather than knew—opposed to his marriage with herself. She was convinced that he considered her not sufficiently well off or important to be a suitable match for his ex-ward. He would assist to rouse Waring's wrath against her, and would not let him lower himself by a personal interview.

She strove to swallow a morsel or two of the dinner set before her; she tried to gather the sense of an agonising tale in the *London Reader*, and interest herself in the tremendous persecutions of the heroine. All in vain. Time, however, was rolling on; she might soon expect Madame Debrisay. Four o'clock struck when she had gone into the bedroom to seek for some piece of fancy work (which Madame Debrisay infinitely preferred to mending her clothes), when the sound of the front-door bell, followed by a step in the next room, made her hope that her kind hostess had returned. Going quickly in to greet her, she beheld Jane, the servant, in the act of lighting the gas, while by the window, looking paler—sterner than she thought he could, stood Leslie Waring!

'Good-morning,' he said stiffly. 'I thought I should find you in.'

This while Jane pulled down the blind and retired. Then he made a step forward to where Mona stood, motionless—her trembling hands locked together, her eyes wide-opened, gazing at him.

'Do you seriously mean what you have written here?' he asked, in a thick, unsteady voice, as he drew forth and opened her letter.

'Yes,' she said; 'I do.'

'Then I have a right to ask the reason of this sudden change. What have I done to deserve it?'

'You have deserved nothing but good and gratitude from me,' faltered Mona, sinking into a chair, for she felt her limbs unable to support her.

'Then why do you desert me?'

'I told you in my letter—the whole truth; I can *not* love you as a wife ought to love.'

'We agreed to get over that difficulty. I hoped to win your affection, *if* you were quite free from any other attachment.'

'And I *am*, Mr Waring! There is not a man in existence whom I would accept at this moment. But'—she was growing calmer under the desperate ne-

cessity of explanation—' I also told you
—what, indeed, I blushed to write—that
my grandmother's wish, her overpowering
need, induced me to consent to what,
otherwise, I should not have accepted.'

' I understand. Then, Mona, you
have treated me very badly. You took
me when I was necessary to you; you
throw me aside when you think you
can do without me! And I love you
so! I thought I was going straight
into heaven when you promised to be
my wife! I had faith in your promise
to try and love me; and, after all, you
were only sacrificing yourself to main-
tain your grandmother—a sacrifice you
gladly escape as soon as you can! You
have broken your contract!'

' You are justly angry. I cannot de-
fend myself. But do you not think you
will be happier with some woman fairer
and better than I am, who will love you
heartily, and—'

' No one will ever be so fair and good
as you seem to me; and as you reject
me, how am I to believe that anyone

will love me? You had every reason to
love me, yet you could not.'

' Love cannot reason.'

' Then you know what love is?' cried
Waring sharply. ' There is something
still in your heart which you will not
speak out! Ah, Mona! why can I not
please you? Why are you so cruel?
You have destroyed my life!'

There was such passionate despair in
his voice that Mona was profoundly
moved. That she had cruelly, selfishly,
wronged him was borne in upon her
with constraining force. She felt guilty,
culpable, to the last degree; and waver-
ing in her resolution,—wishing, if possible,
to do the right thing, she stammered,—

' If—if you think it worth accepting,
I will retract that letter, and—and do
my best.'

' No!' interrupted Waring, with a
dignity of which she did not imagine
him capable. ' You cannot endure me!
I do not want a victim! I love you
too well for that. But, ah, Mona, it is
an agony to think you will have to face
the roughness of life! Whether you love

me or not—whether you desert me or not—I would gladly give half I possess to shield you from all you dare to face. Promise you will let me help you if you need help—promise, Mona!'

'Surely,' she cried, greatly touched— 'surely Heaven has cursed you with something of a woman's heart, or you would not feel so tenderly and generously for one who has pained and wounded you! I feel your superiority, and I humbly beg your forgiveness. I will always think of you as a true gentleman. May you find greater happiness than I could bestow. Here— take this back!'

'Pray keep it,' he said, as she held out her engagement ring of diamonds.

'I cannot, Mr Waring; you *must* take it back!'

He thrust it on his finger.

'Then it is all over between us!' he said passionately; 'all quite over! Perhaps it is better so. It would have broken my heart to try in vain to win your love; and, dear as you are, I would not have you without it. Good-bye, Mona! you

have taught me how unlovable I am;
yet I might have made you happy.'

With a slight despairing gesture of the
hand he turned and left her.

Left her in a state of terrible agitation
and doubt.

She did not expect to be so completely
routed, so utterly ashamed. He was
stronger and nobler than she thought.
She had broken with him, and she had
lost him. She had offered to retract, and
he had rejected her.

It pained her infinitely to think that his
opinion of her had been lowered,—that
she had been so faithless to her promise.

Yet she knew that had she renewed,
or kept to the engagement, she would be
miserable.

' He will forget me soon,' she told herself. ' To-day his bearing was dignified
and earnest, his feelings were deeply
moved—to-morrow, his eye will be caught
by some one of the many charming girls
he meets, and he will be far happier than
with one whose heart is dead, like mine.'

She sat long quite still, thinking painfully, confusedly. Then she nerved her-

self to seek her writing materials, and
begin a letter to Lady Mary.

What a task it was. How worthless and
ungrateful her own conduct seemed to her
as she strove to explain it and excuse
herself. How insufficient, how puerile
her objections must seem to those who
had not the key to the puzzle—that key
none should ever get. She knew that
had she never met Lisle, had she been
heart whole, she might have grown to
like Waring sufficiently well to be happy.
But Lisle had lifted a corner of the veil
which hides the mysteries of life from
young eyes, and given her a glimpse of
human passion and the enchantment of it;
—now nothing less glowing could satisfy
her—all else was tame and weak. And
this hero whom she had invested with
all the attributes of noblest manhood,
strength, and tenderness, the masterful
decision of a fine intellect, the gentleness
of a knight-errant, he had shown himself to her in his true colours, and swept
away the illusions which had gathered
round his image in her mind for ever.
She said truly there was not a vestige

of love in her heart for any man, nor did she believe she could ever believe in another.

She did not dream of the enormous recuperative powers which youth possesses. Still it was a bitter blow, that sent her reeling back from the threshold of life, to recover as best she could her vanished hopes of truth and tenderness —respectful love, everlasting constancy.

She had not completed her difficult letter, when Madame Debrisay came in.

' I am quite done up!' she cried. 'Such vile weather! I will change my boots, and be with you in a minute. But I have a new pupil, so my Wednesdays will be well filled at Kensington. We'll talk over everything at tea.'

The kindly woman's horror and amazement when Mona disclosed the dreadful fact that Waring had come to answer her letter in person, and had gone away in sorrow and indignation, can be better imagined than described.

She was too deeply affected for speech. She pushed back her chair from the table, and sat a silent image of grief.

'And is there nothing to be done!' she ejaculated. '*Dieu des Dieux!* It was my last hope, that when he came himself and you saw him face to face, drowned in sorrow, you'd have given way. How had you the heart to refuse him again?'

'But he did not ask me, dear Deb. He very properly said he did not want a victim. I think more highly of him than I ever did before; but I am sure I have done right in acting as I have, and he will thank me yet!'

'It is a downright tempting of Providence. Ah! Mona, you'll rue the day yet. And to make me post that letter! Ah! if I had known what was in it, I'd have torn it into smithereens before your face. What will become of you now? Everyone's hand will be against you.'

'Except yours, dear friend.'

'I tell you what. My hand is just itching to box your ears, though it will never put you from me. If I only knew the truth. You are keeping back something—I know you are. Ah! and Sir Robert Everard. Won't *he* be in the fury, and Lady Mary. Well, well! I've had many a sore disappointment; but I think this is about the worst. If your poor dear grandmamma could look from her grave—I mean down from heaven —I wonder what she would say!'

'Enlightened as she probably is by the knowledge of another world, she would, no doubt, approve of what I have done.'

'It would be queer knowledge!'

For the rest of the evening Madame Debrisay kept silence, or nearly complete silence, which was, of course, pain and grief to her—while Mona finished and despatched her letter.

In due time it was answered, in rather a distracted fashion, by Lady Mary. She said she thought dear Mona must be under the influence of temporary insanity; that Sir Robert was going up to London to see what was really the matter; and that she prayed Heaven there might not be any secret mischief at the bottom of this unfortunate affair.

The idea of facing Sir Robert alone was too much for poor Mona.

'He will certainly be here to-morrow.

Could you manage to stay at home, dear, dear Deb?' she said imploringly.

'Well, and I don't wonder you are frightened to see him! He will be like a raging lion — small blame to him! There, don't turn so white. I am a bit of a wild beast myself to speak so harsh to a bit of a girl like you! If I did not dread a hard, poverty-stricken life for you, I wouldn't be so mad. God knows, if my own baby girl had lived, I couldn't love her better than I do you! Yes, I will stay by you, my lamb. It will be a tolerably free day to-morrow. I'll write and put off my early lessons, for you may be sure he will come up hot foot the first thing in the morning to row us out of the place.'

This assurance was some stay to Mona. She was very low—she had been for some time unable to eat, and her nerves had suffered severely from the shock of her grandmother's sudden death. It made Madame Debrisay's soft heart ache to see how thin and white her pet pupil had grown, how she started and trembled at any sudden noise, and, above all, at her

steady effort to be calm and helpful. It
was almost too much for her, this waiting
for what the morrow should bring forth.
She knew Sir Robert, though kind, was
choleric, and, like all sensitive creatures,
she shrank from rough words; she strove
to strengthen herself by reflecting that she
was the best judge of what was best for
her own happiness,—that she had a right
to decide for herself,—that she was not
bound to obey Sir Robert, though she
hated to contradict him.

Madame Debrisay put on her best black
silk dress, and a pretty little morning cap
of Brussels lace, in honour of the occasion ;
and Mona swept away the confused mass
of papers into the bedroom, and put the
place into order, adding a few Christmas
roses and geraniums, which she had persuaded Madame Debrisay to let her buy.
She knew how revolted the orderly baronet would be by any untidiness or a
sordid lodging-house look, and she had a
vague fear that he might take her from the
asylum she had sought.

As Madame had anticipated, Sir Robert
came between eleven and twelve. A

glance at his broad, usually good-humoured face, showed how great was the
wrath he had accumulated.

He came abruptly into the room, and
without a word of greeting, exclaimed,—

' What the deuce is the meaning of your
extraordinary conduct, Mona ? Have you
quite lost your senses ? '

' No, Sir Robert. I have been making
up my mind to break off my engagement
ever since my grandmother died,' she said,
gaining courage when absolutely under fire.

' By George ! you ought to be ashamed
to confess it. To throw off a young
fellow that is a great deal too good for
you, the moment a pressing necessity was
removed. I never was so humiliated in
my life as when Waring came to speak
to me last night. You have settled yourself in his estimation : there will be no
drawing him on again—a pretty position
you have landed us all in. What's to
become of you, I'd like to know ? '

' I will try to take care of myself and
not to trouble anyone.'

' Take care of yourself ! Why, you
have acted like a perfect idiot.'

'Well, Sir Robert,' put in Madame Debrisay, 'I must say it is the first time Miss Joscelyn has ever been told so! Marriage is a very serious undertaking, and though it might have been more satisfactory to her friends if she had married Mr Waring, she has a right to do what she feels is best for her own happiness, and Mr Waring's too.'

Sir Robert Everard stared at her, with a 'Who are *you?*' expression, as if amazed at her daring to speak.

'Oh, indeed! Perhaps she is acting under your advice?'

'No, indeed, Sir Robert! Madame Debrisay has been dreadfully angry with me. I confess I deserve that you should all be angry with me; still I do not regret what I have done.'

'I haven't patience to listen to you, and— and I wash my hands of you. I don't suppose Waring would accept any overture now.'

'And I shall certainly not make any,' said Mona quickly.

'Then what is to become of you? You haven't a rap, and my doors shall be closed against you!'

'But mine are open to her,' said Madame Debrisay, with dignity.

'I suspect, and I told Lady Mary so,' he continued, without heeding her, 'that there is some clandestine love affair under all this. You have inherited your mother's taste for a low-born lover.'

'If I find as good a husband, I shall be fortunate,' cried Mona, with spirit; 'nor should *I* be marrying beneath me. *I* have no wish to deny my kind, good father.'

'Then, why did you drop his name?'

'I did not; poor grannie called me by my second baptismal name before I knew what a surname meant; but from this time forward, I will resume my father's.'

'But you are known as a connection of my wife's. I will not have you disgrace us; and I will not support you, unless I know we shall be spared that—'

'Disgrace you, indeed!' cried Madame Debrisay. 'Who mentions disgrace in the same breath with Mona's name. You are forgetting yourself, Sir Robert! You may have a right to be angry perhaps, but don't let your anger make you forget you are a gentleman.'

'By George! it's enough to make a saint swear, to see you prefer a place like this to a good position. I can't take the charge of your future! You are too headstrong; and, after Lady Mary and myself, Mona, you haven't a friend on earth!'

'I suppose *I* count for nothing?' said Madame Debrisay. 'I am certainly a mere roomkeeper. I can't offer my dear young friend the splendours of Harrowby Chase, but I have an unblemished character, and owe no man a farthing. I work for my living, and I make it independently. Moreover, I can put Mona in the way of doing the same, if she is in earnest. Though I am not worth a word or a look, my ancestors were Norman knights when I daresay yours herded their cattle, Sir Robert Everard; so your young kinswoman *has* a friend on earth, besides yourself and her ladyship.'

Sir Robert looked at her amazed, then

in a changed tone, and with a gleam of amusement in his eyes, he said,—

'If I seemed rude, I regret it. Your young friend's unprincipled conduct to a worthy gentleman—who interceded for her, madam, absolutely interceded for her —has irritated me beyond endurance.'

Madame Debrisay bowed her forgiveness.

'I only wish to stay here, and to be forgotten,' said Mona.

Sir Robert played with his watch-chain for a minute in silence.

'I believe it would be best,' he said a last. 'I renounce you from this time forth, nor will I allow Lady Mary nor my girls to hold any communication with you. I have a couple of hundred pounds still in my hands of Mrs Newburgh's money, after paying funeral expenses and other things. I will send you a cheque for it, and whatever belongs to you at the Chase.'

'I have already put everything together, anticipating this expulsion,' said Mona.

Sir Robert made a step or two towards the door, and paused irresolute.

'I'll give you another chance. Will you authorise me to make overtures to Waring? I'll do my best for you, if you will.'

'It is impossible I could consent to such a proposal!' cried Mona.

'Then I have no more to say, nor shall I ever see you again if I can help it.'

He turned to go.

'Though you are so angry, Sir Robert, I am not the less grateful for all your kindness,' sobbed Mona. 'I do love Lady Mary and Evelyn dearly: it is a cruel punishment never to see them again.'

'I have no patience with sentimental bosh,' he returned harshly. 'Your action proves how much of real regard you have for any of us.' And seizing his hat he left the room.

The next instant they heard the front door shut violently, and saw him walk rapidly down the road.

CHAPTER VII.

A NEW LIFE.

'SO that's done,' said Madame Debrisay, stirring the fire with some force, and putting down the poker with a clang.

'How awfully angry he is!' exclaimed Mona, still standing where Sir Robert had left her.

'My dear,' returned Madame Debrisay, 'he is a brute. He might be angry—*I* am angry; but he had no business to speak as he did; and *I* might have been the wall, for all the notice he took of me. I trust and hope he will not do you out of any money you ought to have.'

'Oh, Deb! how can you think of such a thing? Sir Robert Everard is the soul of honour, though he is rather hasty in temper.'

'When people lose their tempers, they often lose their heads and their sense of justice. You may be foolish—I don't deny you are—but I cannot bear to see you crushed and miserable.'

'I am unhappy, but I am not quite crushed. It rouses me to hear people talk as if there was no chance of salvation for me except as Leslie Waring's wife. I am young and willing to work; why should I not earn my living independently, as you said?'

'Why, of course I spoke up bold to that tyrant; but between you and me, the beginning is awful hard work. Still I have an idea. You must wait till I think it out. Meantime, I must go; and you, dear, just take a book, and lie down on the sofa and try to sleep. No one can keep their wits clear when they feel weak and worn out. Then if I can get back in time, we'll have a walk. You must get acquainted with this neighbourhood.

.   .   .   .

An awful quiet settled down on Mona after these agitating interviews. There was nothing more to do,—nothing more to be resisted. She did not regret what she had done, but the reaction was profound. A great gulf seemed to have yawned between her present and her past, which nothing could bridge over.

Her boxes arrived from Harrowby Chase, and a formal list of disbursements on account of the late Mrs Newburgh from Sir Robert Everard, accompanied by a cheque for a hundred and fifty-three pounds, thirteen and fourpence, the balance due to her.

'There, dear Deb, there is my whole fortune! What shall I do with it?'

'We must take care of it, *ma belle*—great care. Let me see. I had better lodge it to my account, and I will give you an acknowledgment that I owe you that amount. I am proud to say I *have* an account at a bank. Began with the Post Office Savings Bank, dear; but as my connection grew, through your dear grandmother and others, I gathered enough to move a step higher. I make

a fair amount for four months of the year
—more than I ever hoped to do once—
then rather less for four more—a trifle
for two—and two don't count at all. If
my health is spared, I hope to provide for
my old age.'

'I know you are a wonderful woman,
dearest Deb. But I cannot live upon
you. What scheme had you in your head
for me the other day?'

'I will tell you. Now I am getting a
name, people begin to bother me to teach
quite little children, and I believe I have
reached that point where a few airs would
do me good. So I shall say I cannot
undertake children under—oh! I'll fix an
age by-and-by; but that I should like
them to be trained for a year, or whatever
time it suits to say, by my pupil and
assistant; that I will see what progress
they are making occasionally, and that
they may be considered as under my
tuition, though at half-price. It will
take, my dear, like wildfire. You are
a very fair musician. We'll go into
partnership, and make a good thing of
it.'

'What a splendid idea! Do you really think I can teach?'

'Not a doubt of it; but I can tell you it's horrid work, and needs the patience of Job. I begin to believe there is nothing on earth so rare as a good ear! You will get on, I am certain, only don't be too anxious, and be sure you give yourself airs. The public is a nettle that stings if it is too tenderly touched.'

'I am not naturally meek, but I shall certainly feel anxious.'

'Have faith in yourself, dear; it's the only way to get on. Then you have a bit of money for present use, and a splendid lot of clothes. You shall pay me for your board when you begin to earn two guineas a week. Then we'll do well. Though you were made for a different life, and so was I, dear—very different. I was the belle of Ballykillruddery, when it was headquarters for the district, though I say it that should not. Ah, well, God's will be done! Who knows what good fortune is in store for you. I can tell you, you are in luck to have your troubles early; mine didn't

begin rightly till I was eight-and-twenty
—over twenty years ago—and now the
best hope is to make enough to die
easy. Whereas there's a chance still
of the beautiful young prince turning up
for you.'

'Not nowadays, dear Deb! And when
do you think I may begin my battle for
independence?'

'I spoke about you last week to
Mrs Mathewson. Her eldest daughter
screeches under my direction : I *cannot*
keep her voice down ; and there's a little
thing of ten she wants me to take for the
piano. Now I'll hand *her* over to you—
they are rolling in riches! Here's a book
on teaching the piano, in German. You
study it, and follow it. Practise up a few
of your noisiest pieces. People seem to
think you can teach music with your
fingers, instead of your head. They are
so taken with a few gymnastics on the
keyboard.'

'Yes, Deb, I will practise diligently.
I haven't touched the piano since poor
grannie died.'

'Well, it's time you began. You have

a pretty touch and a fluent finger. As
to singing; come, let us try that duet
Signor Boccaricho taught you last winter.
What ages away that winter seems to
have gone.'

'Ah! does it not?' said Mona, with
a deep sigh.

And all the glorious spring-time which
succeeded it; the dawn of dazzling delight
when she first perceived that Lisle
quietly but persistently sought her; the
charm of the delicious secrecy which
wrapped their mutual, silent understanding; the history of those few
months which had been the cul-
mination, so far, of her life, flashed
through her memory — clear, vivid, in-
stantaneous. But she turned resolutely
from the picture.

'Where is the book?' she asked.
'I will begin my preparations at once.
I must do credit to your recommenda-
tion. I long to make a start in real
life.'

Reality is a serious thing, yet it has
its inspirations. The sense of doing
real work, — of earning hard money,

has a dignity in its laboriousness which scarcely anything else bestows; and Mona would have rejoiced in this new development of energy, had she not been so deeply wounded. Her sudden, complete renunciation by her valued friends at Harrowby Chase cut her to the soul, especially as she felt she had in a measure deserved it. Her bitter disappointment in Lisle was more regret for the loss of an illusion than sorrow for a personal bereavement. In her short experience of society, she had no friendships or intimacies save with Sir Robert Everard's family. It was this abandonment that depressed and saddened her. Her upbringing had not been luxurious. Mrs Newburgh was a strict economist, though a flavour of stateliness pervaded her life; moreover, Mona had been old enough to know there was a degree of uncertainty about her position and her future before her grandmother had finally and completely adopted her. Yet the life of that one season had been delightful. Mona's was an imaginative and poetic nature, though not without its practical side. The brilliant and beautiful surroundings of the society to which her grandmother belonged charmed her senses, and she had not seen enough of it to perceive the deficiencies which appertain to it as to all human growths. There was, however, a sound, true heart under her fair, quiet exterior which made a home, however homely, not only bearable, but likeable, were love only an inmate to bind the inmates together with the golden links of tender sympathy. Then came the balm of constant employment. What a blessing was enfolded in the divine decree, 'In the sweat of thy brow, shalt thou eat bread.'

It was a curious, trying sensation the giving of her first lesson. If the well-dressed, demure little damsel to whom it was administered only knew how awfully afraid her elegant-looking teacher was of her, all chance of discipline would have been over. But silence, backed by gravity, is a splendid cover for nervousness; and Mona did not utter a word beyond what teaching required, nor did she ever feel the same panic again.

'She has beautiful frocks, mamma,' was the sentence of the little ten-year old. 'Her black cloth must be tailor-made—it fits like a glove; and she has *such* beautiful jet ear-rings!'

Nor did the young lady doubt that a music-teacher so attired must be deserving of all attention.

So the new life was fully inaugurated soon after Christmas — that Christmas which poor Leslie Waring had hoped would be so heavenly bright — which Madame Debrisay and Mona quietly and sadly celebrated together. The former—who was a Catholic if she were anything — accompanied her young *protégée* to church, and enjoyed a particularly crisp French novel over the fire for the rest of the day; while Mona sat long at the piano, playing from memory and dreaming over the past. She gave few thoughts to the future.

'And,' thought Madame Debrisay, 'she might be dining in splendour—in Paris, or Rome, or London—with powdered flunkies behind her chair; not that there is much comfort to be got from *them !* Well, well, there's no accounting for a young girl's whims; but I'm as sure as I am sitting here that there's another man in the case, and, please God, if nothing is said she'll forget him.'

So the days and weeks flew past, and Mona, with the blessed facility of youth, began to revive. A simple life, plenty to do, the society of a kindly and amusing companion, are wholesome tonics. Madame Debrisay was extremely amusing. She had been largely educated by observation. She was at once sceptical and credulous: her mind was utterly untrained — yet a certain keen mother-wit and largeness of heart made her judgment, on the whole, clear. She was still quick in temper, though it had been much chastened, and also extremely resentful of small slights.

Now it so happened that the gentleman who occupied the drawing-room floor had a pet dog—a rough terrier—which he firmly believed was of the true

'Dandie Dinmont' breed, and which madame pronounced to be a 'thorough-bred mongrel.' It was an ill-tempered brute, and used to attack the house cat, which Madame Debrisay had taken under her protection. Dandie, as the dog was called, more than once pursued the cat into madame's sacred apartment, and on one occasion had worried a small fur rug, by which she, for some reason, set great store.

A wrathful message had therefore been despatched to the owner, requesting him to keep his favourite chained up, as he had destroyed some valuable property. The reply—which was no doubt never intended to meet Madame Debrisay's ear—was to the effect that Mr Rigden was 'Willing to pay half-a-crown for any twopenny-halfpenny damage inflicted on her rags and jags.' This was intolerable; the blood of all the Debrisays —she was a Debrisay by birth as well as by marriage—rose in an indignant tide at the affront. Madame Debrisay sought a personal interview in the hall; and as Mr Rigden was in a hurry to catch his omnibus, her dignity and stern remonstrance made not the slightest impression. He told her hastily she should not heed the mischievous representations of a servant; that although he had certainly uttered the words attributed to him, he did not mean them to be repeated. He was quite willing to pay for damages, but he would not chain up his dog to please Mrs Debrisay, or anyone else. So saying he departed hastily, and slammed the door behind him.

'The ill-mannered barbarian!' as Madame Debrisay observed to Maria. 'A *roturier*, my dear; a *roturier*, *pur et simple.*'

After this there was a running fire of hostilities, for Madame Debrisay was by no means disposed to turn her cheek to the smiter.

Things had settled down to a regular routine. The depth of the winter was over; Parliament had met, and Mona had nearly as much to do as she could accomplish without fatigue, though she was quite willing to do more. Madame even talked of making a little excursion to the sea-side at the dead season, if things continued to prosper.

Mona was returning late one afternoon, after one of her busiest days. She was weary, but more hopeful, though she was thinking how this time last year she was looking forward to the mingled joy and terror of being presented. It was a little hard to be so suddenly dragged down, and carried away from all the gaieties and pleasures, the society and distinction, that she had enjoyed a few months ago, and to which she felt she should never return. Yet there was no bitterness in her regret; she felt that she was singularly fortunate in having found such a friend and such a home.

Her reflections were suddenly broken in upon by a familiar voice exclaiming,— ' By Jove! it is Mona! Mona Joscelyn!' and she found her further progress barred by Bertie Everard, Sir Robert's only son, who was studying law, having no military proclivities, and thinking legal knowledge would be useful in managing the family estate, which was by no means flourishing under his father's munificent rule.

'Bertie! I never dreamed of meeting you,' as though the ban which had fallen on her had been 'banishment,'— that an encounter between two inhabitants of the same town had been thereby rendered impossible.

'Nor did I. I thought you had emigrated, or been sent to a penitentiary, or some such thing. You see, when anyone drops out of sight in London, it is such a drop in the ocean, that he or she leaves no trace behind. I am quite glad to see you. Come, tell me all about yourself. Evy has wept gallons over you. She wanted to write, and the Lord knows what, but my mother strictly forbade her. You are an awful black sheep, you know—a lost mutton.'

'Of course I am,' said Mona, smiling. She understood her cousin's dry bluntness. 'But you must acknowledge I have kept out of sight and not troubled you.'

'Yes; it is quite true. Now I have met you, I am amazed to find you still exist. How have you managed it, Mona ? '

' Why trouble about details ? I exist, and want nothing—that is enough.'

' Wonderful woman ! Where are you going ? '

' Home.'

' Home ? Is it far ? '

' Not very.'

' Let me come with you.'

' If you like. I am glad to have a chance of hearing about you all.'

This brief colloquy took place on the Broad Walk, Kensington Gardens. Mona was crossing from a house in Queen's Gate, where her last lesson had been given.

Bertie Everard, a tall, thin, bony young man, most accurately got up, and as unlike father or mother as could be imagined, turned and accompanied her towards the Bayswater Road.

' Do you know, you are looking fairly well ? Cheeks not quite so round, eyes a trifle more sombre than they were last year, but you are a pretty— no, a handsome girl still, Mona.'

'I suppose one does not grow old in five or six months.'

'No; but the tradition in our family is that you have been eating the bread of misery, and precious little of that, bedewed with the water of affliction, and—'

'And you were all content that I should, though we were such good friends, and enjoyed so many happy days together.'

'It was all your own fault, you know. You took your own course. I daresay, if you asked her, my mother would have helped you; but she wasn't bound to look you up. Sentimental generosity is out of date altogether.'

'I do not suppose it would have been a weakness of yours, at anyrate. However, you need not fear for me. I get bread enough, and to spare, and very pleasant bread, too. Now, tell me some news. How is your dear mother? She was always so good.'

'She is exceedingly flourishing and busy, for Evelyn is going to be married —very good match—to Lord Finistoun.

He is a pleasant, easy-going fellow,—
rather an ass, but that will suit Evy.
She hasn't much brains herself.'

'She has sense enough not to think
she has all the brains of the family, as
you do, Bertie.'

'Yes, I do, and I am no great things
after all. Your troubles have not taken the
sharp edge off your tongue, Miss Joscelyn,'
he said, laughing.

'There is no Miss Joscelyn now. I
have resumed my poor father's name.
It is more suited to my fortunes and
fancy.'

'By Jove! And what is it? Craig?
Um! It was a queer notion of Mrs
Newburgh's to suppress it. Nobody
cares or thinks about names now, except
for what they are worth on paper? I
suppose you haven't heard or seen any
thing of Waring?'

'No; of course not.'

'Nor anyone else either! Can't think
what's become of him. Some one *did*
say he was training a colt for the Derby.
I daresay he is glad enough now that
you have broke with him. Can't under-

stand why men marry!—must be an awful
bore.'

' I have no doubt he is obliged to me.'

' And *you* are deucedly sorry you gave
him the chance, eh ? '

' You would not believe me if I denied
it.'

' Well, no, I would not, though you are
a rum sort of a girl, Mona. I always
liked you. You say what you think, and
you held your own with that grandmother
of yours, who was as big a tyrant as I
have met. You are a fool, too, in many
ways,—ready to cut your own throat for an
idea ; but there's something taking about
you. I never thought St John Lisle
would lose his head as he did on your
account. He kept it very quiet, but I
saw through him. I see through a great
many things.'

' I never credited you with such powers
of imagination before, Bertie.'

' Oh, don't try that tone with *me*. I
know what I am talking about. Of course
he would only *marry* a woman with lots
of money, as I think you had wit enough
to know. He is enjoying himself in

India. I had a letter from him some time ago,—asked why he had not seen your marriage announced—asked it in a postscript—always a bad sign of womanish weakness. Where do you live, for Heaven's sake? We must be approaching the far west.'

'Do not come any further, Bertie— you will die of fatigue.'

'No, I will not, but you will, if it's a few miles further out ; let me secure a cab, before we leave the haunts of civilisation behind us.'

'I think ten minutes more will bring us to our destination ; but, to copy your own amiable candour, I would rather you did not come. You will only satisfy your curiosity, and carry away materials for a ridiculous description, to make Evy and Geraldine laugh.'

'Why should you begrudge us our innocent mirth ? It is an absurd preju- dice to feel injured by being what is called "turned into ridicule." You have only to show a stolidly indifferent front, and you rob ridicule of its whole power.'

'I wonder how you would like being laughed at yourself, Bertie?'

'Should not mind; but I am not ridiculous—I am too natural, and always say what I think.'

'I often—I mean I used often, to wonder if you are as hard and heartless as you seem.'

'I believe I am; but come on, I am determined to see your lair, and I do not dine till eight, so I have plenty of time.'

'I cannot prevent you, but I do not want you.' They walked a few paces in silence, then Mona asked,—'And is Evelyn happy? Does she seem happy?'

'Happy as a child with a new toy—she and Finistoun make idiots of themselves in the most approved manner. It will be a great piece of news for her this *rencontre* with you.'

'Does she still care for me?'

'She seemed to do so the last time we mentioned you.'

'That was not recently?'—smiling.

'No, not very.'

'I live here,' said Mona, after a short silence, pausing before Madame Debrisay's abode.

'Ah! queer little box.'

'We,' said Mona gravely, 'consider it a splendid residence; pray walk in, as you *will* come.'

'You are horridly inhospitable,' said Everard, laughing, and he followed her into the house.

On opening the door, Madame Debrisay was discovered resting in an arm-chair, beside a table set for tea. Her bonnet lay on the floor beside her, and her thick and undeniably disordered black hair was uncovered.

'This is Bertie Everard,' said Mona quietly; 'Evelyn's brother.'

'Very pleased to see him I'm sure,' said madame, rising bravely to face the intruder, and not deigning to pick up her bonnet. 'Your sister was one of my most charming pupils.'

She fancied the visit was a freewill offering of friendship to Mona, and she was highly delighted with the visitor.

'Oh, indeed!' returned Everard. 'I should not have thought it.'

'And you find your sweet cousin looking well! I have done my best to take care of her.'

'My cousin?' elevating his eyebrows. 'Can you tell me the exact degree, Mona?—first, second, twenty-fifth?'

'Oh! a cousin removed to the vanishing point of relationship. I have not the faintest wish to claim you, Bertie.'

'Really, Mona, my dear, that is not the retort courteous.'

'If you knew Mr Everard better, dear Madame Debrisay, you would know that he despises courtesy in himself and others.'

'I only hate shams,' said Bertie frankly.

'Let me offer you a cup of tea,' said Madame Debrisay, rather scandalised.

'Thank you; I shall be glad of it, after our long, dusty walk. Really, it's not so bad, now we have got here,' looking round with visible examination. 'It is a better room than mine in the Temple!'

' Is that possible ? ' cried Mona.

' And in better order. Did you fasten up that drapery at the back of the piano, Mona ? '

' She did, sir,' said Madame Debrisay proudly ; ' and, if you'd like to know, the stuff is oriental chintz, and we paid four-pence three farthings a yard for it at Whiteley's sale.'

' By George! you don't say so!' He was deeply interested in pounds, shillings, and pence. ' Why, it looks capital.'

So saying, he took the milk jug and peeped into it.

' I regret it is not cream,' said Madame Debrisay, colouring.

' Yes! cream *is* an improvement, but the tea is very good.'

' It would do you good, Bertie, if you would swallow the contents of the jug, provided it supplied you with the milk of human kindness, which you need so much.'

' That's very smart, Miss Craig, but I don't want any such stuff in my composi-tion. Your milky kindly people are gen-erally asses, and are imposed upon right and left. Miss Craig's manners haven't improved since she came to stay with you, ma'am.'

'There is no use in trying to pierce your tough skin, Bertie. The hippopotamus is invulnerable to bullets.'

'Yes, but he is an ugly beast!' added Madame Debrisay, with a gently reflective air.

Bertie laughed, not quite so easily as usual; and there was a pause while he sipped his tea.

'That's rather a good picture,' he said at length, nodding to a portrait of a refined foreign-looking man, with beautiful lace ruffles and cravatte, and a costume of some two hundred years ago.

'It is the picture of M. Le Baron Debrisay de Coulanges, my grandfather's great-grandfather, who led a party of his co-religionists to Ireland, after the revocation of the Edict of Nantes,' said Madame Debrisay, with dignity.

'The deuce he did! what a bad choice. It's a good portrait. French portraits generally are. Who is the artist ? '

' That I cannot tell ; there are only initials on the picture.'

' Pity it hasn't a well-known name on it. It would fetch a good price.'

' No price would tempt me to part with it ! ' cried madame proudly.

' Oh, indeed ! Now, tell me, how do you manage to rub along ? '

' Madame Debrisay and I have entered into partnership ; she takes the big pupils, and I take the little ones.'

' By George ! Does the squalling and strumming pay for all this ? ' waving his teaspoon comprehensively round.

' It does ; but then you must remember it is all in the fourpence three farthings style of expense,' said Madame Debrisay.

' Gad, what heaps of money we waste ! ' exclaimed Everard, putting down his cup. ' What sums my father gets through ! I suppose you never go to parties or things of that kind, so living out here is of no consequence.'

' There are people who give parties, living even here,' said Mona.

'Indeed!'

'Yes, and we sometimes go to the theatre, and enjoy it very much.'

'Well, it's evident you are not breaking your heart, Mona. If you like the theatre, I will send you a box. I know a couple of managers—amusing vagabonds, they dine with me sometimes—so I can ask them.'

'Thank you! We shall be very glad. Now it is half-past six, Bertie; you had better go.'

'Yes, I will. Is there a cab to be had in this neighbourhood?'

'Why not adopt the habits of the country, and try an omnibus; threepence to Tottenham Court Road, a shilling cab fare on to the Temple.'

'Capital idea. Why one might live for half nothing up here.'

'There are no rooms to let in this house, Bertie.'

'That is a pity. Good-morning, Mrs Debrisay; good-bye, Mona.'

'Happy to see you again,' said Madame Debrisay. 'You are really quite a character.'

'What the deuce does she mean?' asked Everard of himself, as he took up his neatly-rolled umbrella, and opened the door, while Madame Debrisay screamed after him to turn right and go on to a large church where the city omnibuses passed every ten minutes.

CHAPTER VIII.

A CHAPTER OF ACCIDENTS.

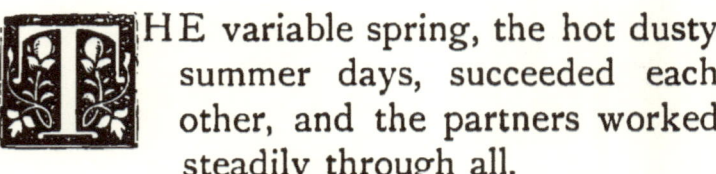THE variable spring, the hot dusty summer days, succeeded each other, and the partners worked steadily through all.

They had gleams of diversion too, for Madame Debrisay had friends and acquaintances of her own profession who often gave her tickets for concerts, and orders for the theatre. These were amusements of which Mona had enjoyed but little during her residence with her grandmother, whose fixed principle it was never to pay for anything of the sort. They were a source of great enjoyment, for Mona was peculiarly alive to beauty, and harmony, and had something of the dramatic gift herself.

With the exaggeration of youth, she reproached herself for being so slight and trivial as to forget too quickly the sorrows and disappointments of the by-gone year. Of all the trials which had been crowded into a few months, the one which came back to her oftenest was her breaking with Leslie Waring. She always wished to hear of him, but he had passed away completely out of her life.

Bertie Everard's remark respecting Lisle's admiration for herself, dwelt long on her mind. There was a certain comfort in it: it soothed her wounded *amour propre* to know that she was not altogether self-deceived. But the impression of St John Lisle was fast fading. Now and then in the park, at the theatre, some soldierly-looking man of fashion would remind her of him, and she thought with a sigh of the difference between the style of such cavaliers and the ordinary toilers with whom it was her lot to associate in future. Still she

began to look at that future with less
of fear than she did, and even ventured
on a little castle building respecting a
visit to Germany next year, for which
she and Madame Debrisay agreed to
'save up,' and not to dissipate any of
their little store in a sea-side trip this
somewhat wet season.

Of course Bertie Everard forgot all
about the orders ; nor did Evelyn pay
the visit Mona looked for so eagerly ;
but the announcement of her marriage
—with a long list of wedding presents,
including ' an Indian shawl from Her
Majesty '—at the end of March, and
her departure for a prolonged tour on
the Continent, explained her non-appear-
ance.

London is a great world. In no
other place can anyone be so success-
fully hidden ; and though Mona moved
about everywhere with a freedom that
was new and delightful to her, she never
encountered her aristocratic relatives but
once, when she saw Lady Mary and
her second daughter driving down Piccadilly. She was, however, lost in the

humble pedestrian crowd, and passed
unnoticed.

A very hot July had driven away
all Madame Debrisay's pupils, save two
or three. The ranks of Mona's were
also thinned, and both were planning a
course of needlework and reading during
the approaching time of rest.

The dog days had compelled their
fellow lodger to muzzle the objectionable terrier—which made him unusually
rampant when the torture was removed
in the house.

Mona had been out one morning to
do some small housekeeping errands as
Madame Debrisay had a headache, and
on re-entering the house with a latch
key, was surprised to hear a sound of
snarling and scuffling in their sitting
room, the door of which was open.
Going in quickly, she beheld Madame
Debrisay, her cap slightly awry, endeavouring to drag a lace shawl from
the fangs of Dandie, who, snarling and
yelping, held on like grim death, stretching the shawl to its fullest length, and
dancing backwards, while she struck at

him ineffectually with a small hearth
brush.

'*Diable de bête!*' she exclaimed. 'Keep
away from him, Mona. I believe he
is going mad.'

'I believe he is only frightened and
angry. Let it go, and probably he
will too.'

This diverting Madame Debrisay's
attention, she relaxed her grasp. The
dog gave a vigorous pull, and trotted
triumphantly with the lace in his mouth
— head and tail erect — into the hall,
where he proceeded to tear it vehe-
mently.

'Just look at that! The only decent
thing I have to put on my shoulders
when I go out. Get away with you,
you cur!'—a thrust of the brush—'Call
him off, Jane!'—another thrust—'Take
that ' — throwing the brush at him
finally.

This routed the foe. He jumped
back, and Mona quickly snatched up
the shawl.

'Me beautiful Chantilly shawl,' almost
wept Madame Debrisay. 'I got it at

a sale the last year you were with us in Paris. Thirty-five francs seventy, and it's worth two hundred! It was as good as new. I will not live in the house with such a brute! He will be tearing our eyes out next! I felt a little better after that cup of tea you brought me, so I did up my hair, and came in. Who should I see but my gentleman perched on the table where I had laid my shawl after folding it up, scratching himself — no less — in the middle of me beautiful lace. I made one dash at it, and tumbled the brute off. Instead of running away, he turned round with real *bourgeois* impudence — like his master's — fastened his ugly teeth in one corner, and would *not* let go.'

'I am sure, ma'am,' said the landlady, coming in, 'I am that sorry — I don't know how to express it. I don't know what's in the dog. He is always trying to run up here, as if he knew it worrited you.'

'I have no doubt he does,' returned Madame Debrisay, examining her lace.

'Look here! There's a tear for you! Here's another! It's just ruined.'

'I think I can mend it, dear,' said Mona sympathetically.

'Now, Mrs Puddiford,' insisted Madame Debrisay impressively, to her landlady, 'I give you your choice — either that savage brute leaves the house, or *I* will.'

'I'm sure, Madame Debrisay, ma'am, it would vex me sore to see you leave. Such a quiet lodger, and sure money. I will speak to Mr Rigden, ma'am, and see if he can send the dog to the country. He is a good lodger too! but that taken up with the dog I don't know he will ever part with it.'

'I neither know nor care,' said Madame Debrisay solemnly. 'I give you two days to expel the venomous cur, at the end of which time, should he remain, consider I have given notice.'

'Dear, dear! why will gentlemen fancy these wild beasts?' almost whimpered the landlady.

'Gentlemen!' repeated Madame Debrisay, with a fine scorn, as she regulated her cap.

'To think how nicely settled I am, with two such first - rate lodgers, and then to think of being upset by a nasty dog. Ah! get out with you!'

This to the audacious animal, who dared to present himself on the threshold with an inquiring look. A violent flick of the duster she had brought, in anticipation of something to be 'wiped up,' again routed Dandie.

'Be sure you explain matters to Mr Rigden *this night!*' said Madame Debrisay, with emphasis; 'and let me know the result. Either he sends away his dog —or goes away with his dog—or Miss Craig and I go, *this day week!*' tragically.

'I will, ma'am!—I will!' sniffed the little landlady. 'I foresee a heap of trouble. Mr Rigden — he is that obstinate and touchy!'

'And you will find I can be touchy too, when I stand on my rights. Now, Mrs Puddiford, I wish to hear no more about this until you bring me your decision to-morrow.'

The landlady retired, pressing the corner of her duster to her eyes; while the yelps of the dog were heard from below, where he was being tied up.

'I think, dear Deb, I saw the very net which would go with the ground of this shawl,' said Mona, examining it carefully, 'at Peter Robinson's; then I could lay the broken pattern over it, and copy it with black filloselle.'

'I'm sure, if anyone could, it's yourself. You have the clever fingers!'

'You see, I did a good deal of lace work at the convent, and other work, in Germany. I am really fond of my needle. I do not even disdain darning stockings, provided they are taken in time; there is something soothing in those long, even lines of running.'

'Well, I am sure you are welcome to mend all mine, for I hate it! But I don't like to see you sitting silent over your stitchery with a pale, sad face, as if you were comparing the present with the past. Ah! it's a terrible change for you!'

'Not half so bad as you imagine,

Deb. The comfort of being with *you* is great; the consolation of being able to help myself is enormous; and at twenty—I shall be twenty in a couple of months—there is so much of life to be explored, that I may find an unexpected oasis! I am not always thinking of the past when I seem in a brown study — I am sometimes speculating on matters that puzzle me, which are probably beyond me, still they have a fascination.'

' What are they, *chérie ?* '

' Oh, there are a great variety of puzzling things. One, for instance, is the awful risk of marrying. It seems to me that the rarest of all qualities in human nature is constancy—yet marriage is for life! Your own character and taste may change several times before you are forty-five or fifty, and how *can* you still love the same person ?'

' Ah, don't talk like a heathen, child! True love grows with your growth and always sees the same charm in the thing it loves — unless, indeed, that thing proves faithless and cruel; even then, some natures cannot be choked off.'

'I cannot understand that,' returned Mona. 'I understand forgiving a great deal—even faithlessness and change—for sake of the old love; but to love anyone who was indifferent to me, seems impossible.'

'Stick to that, my dear; it will carry you safe through a good deal. But I don't think you know much of love, or you'd know, as I do, that it hopeth all things and endureth all things.'

'I can believe that of a mother's—a sister's—a friend's love. But the love of lovers is different. There is a personal feeling in that, which, if it evaporates, can never, I fancy, be recalled; nor do I see that one can complain of its disappearance. There is nothing to be done but to resign it without a struggle, and let one's own passion exhale and die out as fast as possible.'

'I declare, you talk like a book! It's all very fine; but it's natural feeling, not reason, that rules such matters—and so much the better for us poor miserable creatures. Yours is a man's creed—not a woman's, dear. Men never will be constant.'

'Very likely not! Then another tremendous puzzle is life. Why are we sent here to endure so much certain pain—to taste such uncertain joy?'

'You are getting beyond me altogether! Good men tell us, to work out our salvation.'

'Yes, good men of *your* church; but mine says that I never can! — that a mental act of faith—which to many minds is impossible—will do more at the last moment than a lifetime of tender consideration for others—of self-sacrifice —of purity.'

'*Par exemple !* You would make a first-rate Catholic, Mona. I am no great things myself, but I would be proud to see you in the true Church. Ah, there's nothing like it, as churches go! God forgive me, I haven't been to confession for a year and more!'

'Never mind, dear Deb; your goodness to me will more than make up for that omission. But there is small chance of

my becoming a Catholic; can you not
see that?'

'No, I can't. I tell you what I can
see, that although you are an angel to
me, there is a good dash of his Satanic
Majesty in you.'

'Perhaps there is. So be it, if it
will help me in the battle of life! As
far as I can see, the one unpardonable
sin of life is poverty.'

'Of life, Mona? No; of society.
Yes, life is world-wide, society is a corner — often a shabby corner. Faith,
dear, you and I are a brace of philo-
sophers; only we are too wise to have
a theory. Here's dinner; I hope it
will be more digestible than your doc-
trines.'

The next day was stormy, with heavy
thunder-showers, and Madame Debrisay
would not hear of Mona taking a journey
to town in search of materials to repair
the damage done by the delinquent
Dandie. Moreover, a council of war had
to be held.

Mr Rigden was observed that morning
to draw his umbrella from the stand with

a degree of violence which upset all the other umbrellas and sticks, and 'banged' the front door with a recklessness which was in itself a *causus belli*. Soon after, Mrs Puddiford appeared with a rueful countenance.

'Well'm, I have spoken to Mr Rigden. He is noways inclined to hear reason!'

'He wouldn't be a man if he did, unless it were on his own side!' ejaculated madame.

'He spoke most disrespectful,' continued the landlady, beginning to play with the corner of her apron. 'He said he would stand no more d—d nonsense (them was his words, ma'am), and was sorry he had just begun a month, as he would have to pay for it (he is a monthly tenant); that he would look out for rooms, and as soon as ever he found another place, free from cantankerous old women, he'd leave, if he forfeited a fortnight's rent. I am sorry to say he so far forgot himself, but them was his very words, ma'am.'

'I assure you, Mrs Puddiford, it is not of the slightest consequence whether Mr

Rigden considers me old and cantankerous
or not. I congratulate *you* on getting rid
of a troublesome, ill-bred inmate!'

'Well, that may be; but it is hard to
lose six pounds a month!'

'Very well, Mrs Puddiford, if you prefer
it, *we* will turn out, and leave Mr Rigden
to make a menagerie of your house!'

'No, Madame Debrisay; far from it!
You and Miss Craig are real ladies, and I
would be grieved to see you leave; only
six pounds are six pounds, and there is the
dead season coming on!'

'Season indeed! Do you fancy the season affects an out-of-the-way population of
clerks and teachers? Miss Craig and I
will look out for you, and praise you up to
the skies as the best of landladies, which
you are!'

'I am sure, ma'am, you are very good,
and I believe you are lucky! I am not
sorry Mr Rigden is going, only for the
money! He was desp'rate partic'lar, and
the dog *is* a hindrance!'

'Of course it is—shocking brute! We
will do our best for you, Mrs Puddiford.'

' I am sure,' added Madame Debrisay, *sotto voce*, when Mrs P. had gone, ' I hope I'll succeed, for if her rooms remain empty she'll think I have lost her her six pounds a month, and " there will be wigs on the green ! " '

' I hope nothing disagreeable will arise, for I have grown quite at home here ! ' exclaimed Mona.

' That man had a nice little room above stairs for his lumber. If I could get her a good lodger at six pounds a month without it, she might let you have it for a song,' said Madame Debrisay reflectively.

' Ah, Deb, you are a profound schemer ! '

.   .   .   .

The next day was bright and fresh after the thunder, and Mona having given a lesson in Gloucester Place early in the afternoon, went on to Regent's Circus to match the lace, intending to make madame's shawl as good as new.

Having done her shopping, she crossed to the other side, and walked a little way towards Tottenham Court Road, hoping to find room in an omnibus, without having to struggle at the regular stopping-place. Presently a Royal Oak omnibus came up, and paused before she hailed it. Mona hastened to enter as soon as an elderly and somewhat decrepit-looking man had descended, with the help of a stick and a baggy umbrella.

The omnibus moved on before the old gentleman had one foot clear of the step, and he fell prone on the damp, profusely watered ground. The driver of a hansom could hardly draw up quickly enough to prevent his horse from trampling on the prostrate figure, which seemed unable to recover the perpendicular.

Mona, by a natural impulse, bent down to assist him, and a burly policeman soon set him on his feet.

' No bones broke,' he said cheerfully, feeling his legs and arms. ' Here's your stick and umbrella. You go into the confectioner's there, and take summat. You'll be as right as a trivet in five minutes.'

So saying, he proceeded on his stately march, leaving the sufferer standing, with difficulty supporting his trembling self on his stick, and looking round him with a pitiful expression of bewilderment.

'I am afraid you are hurt?' said Mona kindly. She did not like to desert him, for she felt he was not a Londoner.

'I've just an awfu' pain i' my back,' he said pantingly, 'and feel dazed like. If I could sit doon a bit.'

'Come into this shop and have a glass of water;' and she guided him to a pastry-cook's close by, where she found a chair, and feeling alarmed at the old man's extreme pallor, asked if he would not try a little brandy and water.

'Ay,' he said; 'I must have something to raise my heart!'

His eyes closed partially, and Mona begged an attendant to bring the restorative. Her patient was a small, spare man, with thin grey hair, small whiskers, faded blue eyes, a contemptuously up-turned nose, and a wide, thin-lipped mouth. He was neatly dressed in a pepper-and-salt coloured suit, and though not a gentleman, was by no means of the workman class, nor yet like a city clerk.

'Try and take a little of this,' urged Mona.

'Thank ye, thank ye.'

He put the glass to his lips and drank very slowly. 'The Lord be thankit,' he said, placing it half emptied on the table, 'for saving my life; but I am sair shaken!' Again he drank. 'Ow!'—he uttered a strange sound between a groan and a sigh. 'It was near a' ower wi' me! I am much beholden to you, my young leddy. I must try an' get awa' to my bed, but I can scarce stan'. I had better get into a cab.'

'You had better rest a few minutes first,' said Mona, who felt sincere compassion for him. 'I am afraid you are more hurt than you think.'

'I am a puir frail bodie. Eh, but my back is twisted! What'll they ask now for a cab'—he called it a 'cawb'—'to Camden Town?'

'I am not sure—eighteenpence or two shillings.'

'It's a cruel, costly place; but,' apologetically, 'I canna' help it; I'll just pay for the spirits and water, and gang my lane.'

He dived into a side pocket—he routed out his trouser pockets—his breast pocket —all in vain.

'Guid preserve us!—it's clean gane! My pocket has been picked!'

'Oh! that is dreadful! I hope you had not much in it?'

'Too much to lose! A bit gold, half-a-crown, and a saxpence. Now I canna pay for my drap o' speerits.'

'That is a mere trifle—I will pay for it.' Going to the counter, she said,—'This poor gentleman's purse has been taken, I must pay for what he has had.'

'I daresay it is an accident that may happen to him again, if he finds kind young ladies to pay for him,' said the buxom woman behind the desk, smiling— 'sixpence, please.'

'Do you feel equal to go home,' said Mona, who was beginning to feel a little ashamed of her Quixotic attentions to this elderly waif. 'I will get you a cab if you like.'

'Wait a bit. Where do you bide? I want to pay ye what you've laid oot.'

'Oh! never mind; it does not matter.'

'Ye are a Scotch lassie?'

'No, I never was in Scotland.'

'Ah! I thocht ye were, from yer bonnie reed heid."

'Indeed!' said Mona, laughing.

She could not bear to have her hair considered red.

'Weel, I'll no leave this till I know where I'll find ye.'

'There is my card then, but I live ever so far away. Pray do not trouble about me; I am very glad to have been of any use to you.'

'Ah! but you were! you have saved my life. If you had not stood between me and that cawb, I'd have been a deid mon! I'll try and get home.'

Struggling to his feet, and seizing his umbrella, he hobbled to the door. Mona followed him.

'You'll hear from me,' said the old man, thrusting the card into his breast-pocket; 'and I'll never forget ye, never. Could you find me a shut-up cawb. I canna bide yon things, wi' the driver stuck up behind.'

'Yes ; there is one!'

A very battered vehicle drew up.

'You drive me to Mrs Smith's, number saxty-sax Carolina Crescent, King's Road, Camden Town—d'ye know it?'

'Yes, sir.'

'What will ye charge?'

'Two and sixpence.'

'Two and sixpence! Whar do you think ye'll go to? Naw, eighteenpence.'

'Ask for his card, and make the people at your house settle it,' suggested Mona.

'Make it two shillin', and I take you safe and aisy.'

'Vara weel. Good-bye, missee; I cannot help thinking you are a Scotch lassie.'

With infinite difficulty and many groans, he scrambled in, dropping his umbrella during the process. Mona picked it up and gave it to him. He seated himself with his back to the horse, smiling and nodding to his young protectress as he drove slowly away.

'What a funny adventure!' thought Mona. 'I wonder if Madame Debrisay will scold me.'

But Madame Debrisay was in a placid

mood when Mona reached home—for
madame had her moods.   She had passed
the morning and some of the afternoon
auditing her own and Mona's accounts.
The result was, on the whole, satisfactory, though,—'The way money slips
through your fingers is most amazing,'
she observed; 'though we have done
pretty well, we couldn't afford a trip
anywhere—not prudently; and *you* cannot
put by anything.   At all events, you have
not reduced your own bit of money much,
that's a comfort; keep a tight hold of it,
dear.'

Having heard her friend's summary, and
assisted to reduce the sea of small account
books, scribbled scraps of paper, bills, and
receipts to something like order, Mona
related her adventure, and madame did
not scold.

'Well it was funny!   Maybe the old
gentleman is a millionaire in disguise!
they are generally queer.   Maybe your
sixpence will prove the sprat that caught
a whale.'

'You have too much imagination, Deb,'
said Mona, laughing.   'There was nothing

of the millionaire about my old man. He was too humble for a moneyed man. If they are queer, they are generally consequential. I fancy he will make his way here. He is very feeble, however, and I imagine "cawbs"—as he calls them— are too costly for his taste. I am almost sorry I gave him my card, but he was quite determined to have it. He seemed so dazed and helpless, I felt grieved for him; but he is not by any means attractive.'

'Well I shall be curious to see what will come of it! It is my belief that your meeting didn't happen for nothing,' and Madame Debrisay shook her head solemnly. 'I believe you are a lucky girl, Mona.'

'Only lucky in having you to befriend me! Your cap is very crooked, dear—go and put on your bonnet! I am not a bit tired. Let us indulge in a hansom to Kensington Gardens, and stroll about till it is time for a late tea.'

From some unrevealed cause, there seems to be a tendency in events to accumulate at intervals, like the seventh wave, which scientists tells us is always the largest. So after the monotonous ripple of many quiet weeks, the crop of incident which has been ripening, bursts its bounds and expends itself in a few days.

The Saturday following Mona's rescue of the old Scotchman, she was surprised and delighted by the receipt of a letter from Evelyn Everard, now Lady Finistoun.

After voluminous apologies for her silence, she expressed her warm sympathy with her 'dearest cousin.'

'They were all so angry with you, that, without giving myself the trouble to think (my usual way, you know), I took for granted that you were a dreadful criminal; still I was as fond of you as ever—but mother would not hear of my writing. Then I was so bewildered about Finistoun. He came and went, and some people thought he was going to marry Lady Georgina Fitz-Maurice; but *I* did not. At last it was all settled; then we were frantically busy, and then I was travelling so much, and so selfishly happy, I never gave a thought to anyone, which is disgraceful, I know. Now, dear, that I am married to the nicest, kindest, pleasantest of men, I feel you were quite right to refuse Mr Waring. Poor man—I liked him very much. It must be quite awful to be united to anyone you cannot love with all your heart. Of course if Mrs Newburgh had lived, it would have been different. I have told Finistoun all about you. He remembers you last year, and admires you very much. He says you are a plucky girl, but does not think you were wise to throw over Leslie Waring. The best of men, dear Mona, have very little sentiment about other people's marriages. Let us hope they have about their own. I do trust you are not very unhappy. Bertie said he met you, and that you were looking well, and seemed quite bright. Are you still living with that nice, pleasant Mrs Debrisay? Pray give her my kind regards. I am sure I used to try her patience. Tell her I had some singing lessons when we were in Milan, and

Signor Squallicini — a great man, I assure you — said I had been very well taught.

'We are getting tired of moving about, and intend returning in August to Scotland. Finistoun has a deer forest in the Western Highlands. We shall be there almost all the autumn. If I can at all manage it, I will come and see you as I pass through London ; and you must come and stay with me. I am sure you will like Finistoun ; he is not exactly handsome, but *distingué*, and really very clever. My father thinks very highly of him ; and he is a sound Conservative. The dear mother is flourishing, and looks forward to presenting Geraldine next season. It is lonely, not having a daughter " out." Good - bye, dearest Mona. You will forgive my neglect, and grant I had a good excuse.—Ever your attached   EVELYN FINISTOUN.'

'I am not so sure about that,' said Mona, smiling, as she put the letter which she had read aloud, back into its envelope. 'But I am most grateful to her for writing at all. She is really a nice, dear thing.'

'So she is. I am glad Squallicini thought she had been well taught. I have heard of him. He gets his guinea a lesson. I daresay I can do just as well, and I thought my fortune made when I first got seven-and-six. Why, Mona, there's a little man trying to open the gate—an old man, with a stick and an umbrella. It must be your millionaire.'

CHAPTER IX.

'OH, MY PROPHETIC SOUL, MY UNCLE!'

IN a few minutes the severe Jane entered, and told them there was 'a—gentleman'—she hesitated before pronouncing the term—'wanting to see Miss Craig.'

'Show him in at once, Jane,' said Madame Debrisay graciously, and the hero of Mona's adventure came in slowly, having left his hat in the hall.

He had rather a low, wide head, and a kind of reluctant smile.

'You'll excuse me,' he said, falling on to a chair, rather than taking a seat, 'but I am varra frail. It's a long way from the station here. I told you, missee, I would not forget ye, and I haven't.'

His exceedingly Scotch accent must be imagined.

'Very pleased to receive you, sir,' said Madame Debrisay blandly.

'But you should not have taken the trouble,' added Mona compassionately.

'I wanted to come,' he said, wiping his brow with a red cotton pocket-hand-kerchief. 'First, I wanted to pay ye back your siller'—he extracted a small bag purse from his trousers-pocket, and took out sixpence; 'and there it is,' laying it on the table. 'Next, I wanted to ask you a few questions, if you don't mind.'

'Certainly not.'

He did not reply immediately, but looked inquisitively and sharply round the room.

'You have a nice, tidy place; a bit of garden is pleasant. It's better, a good deal, than where I am. Maybe it costs more. I pay a guinea a week for a bed-room and share of a sitting-room.'

'We pay very little more for two rooms all to ourselves,' said Madame Debrisay.

'Is she your mother?' he asked, looking at Mona.

'No, not my mother, though she behaves like one.'

'Ah! And are you sure you have no Scotch blood?'

'My father was Scotch.'

He drew forth her card, and looked at it, slowly reading out, 'Miss M. J. Craig.'

'What does the M. and the J. stand for?'

'Mona Joscelyn.'

'They are not varra Christian-like names. Where did your father live?'

'In Glasgow.'

'Ah! And now, what was your mother's name?'

'Newburgh.'

'Ay, just so. Your father's name was John Craig, and he was a clerk in the Western Bank of Scotland?'

'His name was John; but I know little else about him. I remember faintly that he was kind and loving.'

'Well, *I* knew him,—knew him from his babyhood. My name is Craig—Alexander Craig, and I am your father's eldest brother.'

'Indeed!' cried Mona, touched, nay, even pleased, to meet anyone of her father's blood. 'Then you are my uncle, my own uncle!'

'I am that,' he returned earnestly.

'But, my dear sir,' ejaculated Madame Debrisay—'forgive the caution of an old woman of the world — can you supply some proof that you are this dear child's nearest relative?'

'You are right to be cautious, mem. I have a letter from my niece's grand-mother, written near fifteen years ago, offering to take her and provide for her, if her father's people would undertake · never to come nigh her or interfere with her. I was a bachelor, and a busy man. I never approved of my brother's mar-riage. He took a wife from a class that despised his own, so I just let the poor wean go. I loved your father,' he con-tinued, looking at Mona, 'almost like a son. You have a look of him, and a bonnie reed heid like his. Your mother was a pretty, dark-haired lassie;

but I lost him when he married. She was too fine for me, and I lived away from them. Here's your grandmother's letter.' He took out a large pocket-book, from the recesses of which he drew a letter, and, handing it to Mona, observed,—'It's not over ceevil. She is just ane of those aristocrats that think a' the world's dirt but themselves.'

Mona took it, and read the short sharp statement of Mrs Newburgh's requirements, which was addressed to 'Mr Alexander Craig.'

'It is indeed poor grannie's writing,' she said, passing it to Madame Debrisay. 'I am glad to find you, uncle!' and she gave her hand to her new-found relative.

'Thank you!' he exclaimed, holding it a minute. 'It was just the guidin' o' Providence that brought you to yon fearsome street to help me. When I looked in your face, I felt you were nae that strange. But whar's your grandmither?'

'In her grave,' said Mona sadly. 'She died suddenly—in my arms.'

'I hope she was weel prepared! And when was she called?'

'She died last November!'

'Ah, aweel! she'll have fund oot by this time that the poor and lowly of this warld are the elect of the next.'

'Mrs Newburgh was a true Christian and a real lady,' put in Madame Debrisay emphatically.

'They dinna always hang togither,' returned their new acquaintance.

'She was very, very good to me,' said Mona.

'Anyway, you've had a wise-like up-bringing. You are not ashamed of your Uncle Sandy, though he *is* a plain bodie?'

'Ashamed! No, indeed.'

'Now'—he called it 'noo'—'tell me how ye come to be here with this leddy? I thought the Honourable Mrs New-burgh'—with somewhat sarcastic stress on 'the Honourable'—'was to leave you a fortin'.'

'Alas! my dear sir, my dear young friend's story has been a real tragedy,' began Madame Debrisay, who proceeded, with suitable modulations of voice, to 'recite' the tale of Mrs Newburgh's losses, and Mona's consequent poverty—

of the necessity for her labouring in order
to live, and being reduced to her present
position.

Uncle Sandy listened with profound
attention.

'Reduced, ye ca' it,' he said.   'It's
no "reducing" for an honest lassie to
earn her own bread, which is mair honourable than the honours of the peer-
age! So you live here, my dearie! Ah,
there's a good drap of Craig bluid in yer
veins, or you would not have set up for
yourself, like a wise lassie.   If ye can
keep a roof like this over your head, you
canna be doing so bad.'

'Remember my dear Madame Debrisay
pays by far the larger half.'

'And what is she to you?'

Mona explained.

'I think,' said Uncle Sandy, with grave,
deliberate approbation, 'that you are just
a pair of varra honest, respectable women.'

'Thank you, uncle,' said Mona, laughing.
'We are both proud of your verdict.'

'Perhaps,' said Madame Debrisay in-
sinuatingly, 'perhaps your uncle would
stay and share our modest mid-day repast.

We have but a little cold roast beef, a salad, and "*omelette aux fines herbes,*" but at least it will avert the pangs of hunger.'

'*Roast* beef, did you say?' asked Mr Craig anxiously; 'I canna digest boiled! But you're varra good, and I shall be happy to join you, for the pleeshure of your society! As I told you, I am varra frail. I worked hard a' my youth under a fine man, Mr Kenneth Maceachern, of Maceachern & Leslie's, the great jute manufacturers. He retired, but he just missed the occupation, and went off like a puff of wind. I keepit on, and saved a bit, and my old master remembered me in his will, so, as I found my health failing, and new men coming into the firm, I thought I would rest and try to recover. I took a cottage an' a bit farm awa' in the west, but I got rheumatics, and grew worse, so I cam' up to try a great London doctor, and was recommended to yon place in Camden Town. The son of one of our clerks lodges there; but he is out a' day, and I suspect a' the night too. I am just wearyin' o't; but I am not half cured yet.

I wonder now if this place is much further from Harley Street?'

'By no means, my dear sir!' cried Madame Debrisay. 'It is a shorter and a pleasanter drive. I presume you are consulting the famous Dr Swaithem?'

'That's the man. He is awfu' costly.'

'What matter! so long as you can regain your precious health. I think you would find this neighbourhood more salubrious, and in every way preferable.'

'It may be. I will think of it.'

'Will you not take the arm-chair, uncle?' said Mona; 'that is such an uncomfortable one.'

'Thank ye; it's weel thought on.' With various groans and twitches, Uncle Sandy transferred himself to the seat recommended. 'Ye see,' he explained, 'I have been sair afflicted with a weakness in the spine; it's a sore hindrance. I have been nigh a month in London, and I've not heard one of the famous preachers yet. I have not had many opportunities, and I am weel aware of my own defeeciencies; but if it was not for my puir frail body, I could improve myself rarely

in this great cawpital. There's lectures,
and concerts, and sermons, and the
like.'

'But I hope you will get stronger,
uncle; then you will be able to enjoy
this wonderful town,' said Mona kindly,
touched by the poor man's desire to go to
school again in his old age.

Here Madame Debrisay slipped quietly
from the room—to make some addition to
dinner, Mona did not doubt.

'Tell me,' said Uncle Sandy—the hoarse
whisper in which he usually spoke inten-
sified—'tell me, what does she make
you pay her for living here?'

'She does not *charge* me anything. I
pay my share of our food and fire—that is
all.'

'Ah! and she is no of your blood?'

'No; I came to know her seven or
eight years ago, as I told you.'

'It is just wonderful,' he ejaculated, and
sat silent for some time, with a curious,
half-satisfied, half-mocking smile in his
face.

Then the prim figure of Jane appeared,
and she proceeded to lay the cloth.

The dinner was very successful. Uncle Sandy was exceedingly communicative as to what he might and might not eat. At first he said he would take nothing but cold water to drink; then he fancied there was a slight taste—he could not exactly define what—in the water, and when he perceived this, he had always been warned to qualify the water with a drop of spirits. He supposed they hadn't any whisky? No; well he would do with a trifle of brandy. 'The next time I come to see ye,' he said, with an air of great generosity, 'I'll bring you a bottle of real good stuff—it's far wholesomer than brandy.' He seemed to enjoy his repast, and afterwards made many inquiries into Madame Debrisay's history. He was also profoundly interested in the prices current of all articles of consumption in London. Then, noticing the piano, he begged his niece to sing him a song. She complied. Before she was half through it he stopped her by observing that he had an uncommon ear for music, but that it must be Scotch music. So Mona changed her tune to 'Oh! wert thou in the cauld blast,'

which gave him great delight. He nodded
his head and tapped the carpet with his
stick in time to the music, and declared
with feeble energy, that there were no
songs like Scotch songs—no intelligence
comparable to that of Scotsmen — no
church system like that of Scotland.
Then he looked at his watch, and said he
was sorry, but he must leave them ; that it
was the only cheerful afternoon he had
spent since he came to London, and expressed his resolution to look for lodgings
in their neighbourhood.

'Pray, let me get you a cab,' said Mona.
'You will be so very tired walking all the
way to the station a second time.'

'Hoot, toot! I am stronger since lately,
and money is not so plentiful as to let me
hire cabs everywhere I go. Naw, naw.
I'll just walk to the station. I have my
ticket to Gower Street, and I will get on
fine from that for tippence. Good-bye,
my lassie. I'll no forget how ye helpit
your uncle. Good-bye to you, mem.
Maybe you'll help me to find a respectable
lodging. I can't come again till the day
after to-morrow, for I have to see the

doctor; but if it is any way fine, I'll not fail you.'

Mona went out to open the garden gate for him, and watched him hobbling down the road for a moment or two, and then returned to Madame Debrisay.

'What an extraordinary encounter!' cried Mona, throwing herself into a corner of the sofa, and laughing unrestrainedly. 'I imagine Uncle Sandy is a character, and I really am sorry for his ill health and loneliness; but I am afraid he will be rather a bore if he settles near us. He seems to have fascinated *you*, dear Deb.'

'Poor creature. I did feel for him, and I think he is naturally a very superior man. But, Mona, my child, it's for your sake I spoke. Now Providence has thrown him in your way, I don't want you to lose your hold on him. Keep him by you, dear, and he will leave you all his money. No one can provide much for old age by teaching, and you must think of the future, *ma belle.*'

'But how can you fancy he is rich? He is evidently extremely careful of

money, and he did not let fall one word
by which one could be authorised to consider him rich. He may have saved
enough to live on, and pay his doctor's
bill, but that will be about all.'

'Well,' returned Madame Debrisay,
'there is no use arguing about what
neither of us can be sure of. I have my
ideas pretty strong, and I am sure you
are not the girl to turn your back upon a
relation because he is poor.'

'I should hope not indeed!' cried Mona.
'I am quite willing to do my best for the
poor old man ; but he will worry us if he
is anywhere near.'

'It will not be for long,' said Madame
Debrisay soothingly. 'He will be going
back to his place in the west of Scotland
as soon as he is cured.'

'His place,' cried Mona, laughing.
'His cottage and farm, you mean.'

'Never mind. He has enough to move
about with, and pay doctors ; and you
might as well have it after him, poor
fellow. I do not think he is long for
this world.'

Mona laughed more heartily.

'You wicked, grasping Deb!' she exclaimed. 'You want to turn me into a
legacy hunter! I assure you I will be
kind and attentive to my poor father's
brother, whether he has a cottage or a
castle. He will probably not stay here
long, and we may as well make him happy.
He must have had a dull life. It must be
very hard to feel life slipping away before
you have known enjoyment.'

'Ah, my dear, don't you be downcast—
times will mend.'

'Do not fancy I am grumbling. I have
some very bright days to look back upon'
—a quick deep sigh,—'and the present is
far from being unhappy. Only, the Mona
Joscelyn of this time last year has disappeared for ever, and Mona Craig, a
more useful and sensible young woman,
has replaced her.'

'If I could see you rich and free, and
in your proper place, I would die happy;
and who knows I may yet see you get the
better of those cold-hearted Everards.'

'They are not cold-hearted. They
had a right to be angry, and I have
no feeling of resentment against them,

though they *might* have asked what had
become of me.'

'If that is not coldness, I do not know
what is.

.   .   .   .

A few more days brought them to
August. During these days Uncle Sandy
made no sign. Indeed, both Madame
Debrisay and Mona were too much occupied with lessons, some of which were
crowded together to allow of pupils leaving
town, and with their own affairs generally,
to think much about him.

Both partners were looking forward to
the delights of rest well earned. Mona
was quietly but profoundly thankful that
she had not been obliged to earn her
bread among indifferent strangers,—that
she had been supported by the warm
sympathy of a true friend.

Bereft of sympathy, life would be but
a struggling mass of discordant atoms,
without coherence, without harmony. Justice might guide our actions—even generosity might bestow its bounty; yet,
needing that centripetal attraction, human
souls would fly further and further from

each other. Sympathy, too, is the informing soul of genius. The power to put one's self in another's place,—to understand by the magic of fellow feeling his strength and weakness,—to penetrate those dusky mental corners where lurk the meanness and deceit of which he is ashamed, and by which he is nevertheless actuated,—the broad kindliness that disdains no atom of humanity, but sees a possible self in the poorest and most fallen—these bestow the faculty of true second sight on him who perceives much, because he loves much. Madame Debrisay and Mona were happy together, because they thoroughly understood each other.

There were depths in Mona's nature, perhaps, beyond the reach of madame's plummet ; but there was nothing in hers to make it discordant. Indeed, the more it was called upon, the more readily did it respond—as a high-mettled steed answers to the spur, or breaks its heart in the attempt.

Mona enjoyed the pleasure of answering Lady Finistoun's letter. It was so delightful to be remembered after many days.

The last lesson had been given—the last promises to write 'directly they returned to town,' spoken, and Madame Debrisay and her junior partner, meeting accidentally in the train, walked home together.

'I do think,' said the former, 'that ours is the neatest garden in the villas; but I fancy the trees are turning a little already.

'The green has deepened, that is all,' returned Mona. 'Look, Deb! Mrs Puddiford has put up a card. Mr Rigden must be going sooner than we thought.'

'Well, I shall not be sorry, though I must say the dog has behaved very well lately. I will ask Mrs Puddiford to come up after tea. I suppose he is going. I do hope she will let the rooms soon. It certainly is a bad season.'

'Yes; she will fret a good deal if she does not.'

And Mrs Puddiford disclosed a tale of woe.

Mr Rigden had returned early, and informed her that he had found better and cheaper rooms,—that he was going

away to the country the next day,—
that he would take his dog, and would
not return, therefore Mrs Puddiford
might make out his account at once,
as he did not intend to hold any further
communication with her.

'He spoke that disdainful, ma'am,
that I felt choked like! To lose a
good, regular-paying lodger, and him
parting unfriendly, *is* trying.'

'No doubt it is, Mrs Puddiford,
but you will have nearly a fortnight's
rent, and in that time I'll find another
tenant for you. I have one in my
eye.'

'Well'm, and I hope you will succeed,
for the sight of those rooms lying empty
is enough to give me indigestion.'

'Who do you think of, Deb? Not
my uncle!' exclaimed Mona, when the
landlady had retreated.

'Yes, I do, dear. Then I could
keep my eye on him, and it would give
us much less trouble to look after his
little wants if he were in the same
house.'

'Well, really, Deb, I am afraid he

would bore us greatly — though it is rather unkind and selfish to say so.'

'Yes it is, *cherie*, and I am ashamed of you. But let the poor soul have a bit of comfort while he is in this strange wilderness of a place; it will help him to get better all the quicker, and then he will be off to his residence in the west of Scotland. Perhaps he will return our hospitalities, by inviting us to stay with him next year. I'd like a month in the Highlands, and if you will only be guided by me, house and land and all will be yours.'

'House and land! Why, Deb, you are more imaginative than ever. However, do as you like. I am awfully selfish, I am afraid, but I dread that poor Uncle Sandy may spoil our holiday.'

The following morning brought a letter from Mr Craig, written in what had been a business hand, now run to seed, and exceedingly shaky.

He had been, he said, exceedingly unwell, and confined to the house with a bad cold; that he was now considerably better, and proposed calling on Wednesday first,

when he hoped his niece and her friend
—the orthography of whose name had
escaped him—would assist in finding him
suitable lodgings, as his present abode was
cold and damp, and most prejudicial to
his peculiar condition.'

'Wednesday first!' repeated Mona.
'Does he mean Wednesday next?—that
will be to-morrow.'

'He will come just in the nick of
time!' exclaimed Madame Debrisay. 'He
is the very man for the rooms upstairs,
and they are the rooms for him. Now,
leave everything to me.'

'Very well, dear, I know you only want
to serve me.'

Madame Debrisay lost no time in
advising Mrs Puddiford to put the
rooms in order, as it was probable that
a gentleman would look at them next day.

'A very advantageous tenant, Mrs
Puddiford,' added madame, with some
importance. 'He is wealthy, but somewhat eccentric. He does not wish to
be considered poor, or to seem poor—
still he is sound and reliable, and will
be most punctual.'

'I am sure, ma'am, it will be rare luck to let my rooms straight off! and to a relation of Miss Craig's too.'

'I will come up and look at them, Mrs Puddiford.'

'They are all in disorder now, ma'am; but I never let real dirt lay about.'

So Madame Debrisay ascended, and remained some time absent.

When she returned, she took up the needlework she had left, and said gravely,—

'Mona, my heart, write a line to your uncle; ask him to take his bit of dinner with us to-morrow, and mention that there are rooms to let in this house; but if they do not suit him we will look for others.'

'I will ask him to dinner, certainly; but let us leave the question of lodgings to the chapter of accidents.'

'Mona, I feel a conviction that you should not let that nice old man slip through your fingers.'

'Dearest Deb! why do you talk as if you were a greedy legacy-hunter, when you are really the most generous and disinterested of mortals! I will do all I can for my uncle, but I will not let him

interfere with my life—nor would I, if I
believed he had many thousands to be-
queath, which I do not.'

Madame Debrisay opened her lips to
speak, and then closed them firmly, keeping silent for some instants.

' Well, dear,' she said at length, ' maybe
you are right.   I am a little inclined to
follow " Will-o'-the-wisps ; " take your own
way.'

' You are a wise Deb after all,' returned
Mona, going to the writing-table, and
beginning a note to her uncle.   ' Of
course, if he chooses to take the rooms, I
will make no objection.'

' We will go out after dinner,' observed
Madame Debrisay, ' and I'll get some
ribbon for your hat.   You will see if I
don't turn out something equal to Madame
Isabelle.'

' I have no doubt you can—'

And Madame Debrisay glided skilfully
away from the subject in dispute.

' There's " The World," ma'am, just
come in,' said Mrs Puddiford next morning.   ' Mr Rigden, he have left no address, and I think I need not worrit my-

self about it; so I leave it with you to look at.'

'Thank you!' returned Madame De-brisay. 'I daresay there isn't a word of truth in all these papers say; but it amuses one at an idle holiday time to look at it.'

'Yes! poor grannie used to read it, and laugh and grumble all the time. It was amusing to hear her comparisons of the present with the past. She was very clever. She never railed at the differences which had come about. She evidently preferred things as they used to be, but accepted changes as inevitable, and probably improvements for a younger generation.'

'Ah! *ciel!*' interrupted Madame De-brisay. 'Listen to this. It is a paragraph among " What people say " :—

' " Play has been unusually high for the time of year at Monte Carlo. One trio has lost or won large sums, and the *habitués* of the Salle de Jeu have, night after night, hung absorbed on the fluctuations of their fortunes. One of these is a Russian prince, well known in fashionable circles,

both in London and Paris. Another is
an Austrian baron, celebrated for his
theatrical speculations. The third, whose
luck at first astonished the oldest fre-
quenters of these famous rooms, is a young
Englishman of good fortune and respectable connections—Mr Leslie Waring—
whose horse was the favourite for the
Derby, and was so unexpectedly beaten,
seemed to have recovered the favour of
the fickle godess, but has since lost very
heavily. He shows great pluck, and is
said to await with confidence 'the turn of
the tide.'"'

Madame laid down the paper with a
sigh.

'I am sorry for that poor fellow!' she
exclaimed.

'And so am I; heartily sorry,' said
Mona, stopping short in her task of re-
arranging some flowers.

'Ah! if he had had a good wife to keep
him straight.'

'Don't!' cried Mona. 'Don't! I cannot bear it. And you are mistaken, Deb;
it is not my fault. Mr Waring told me
himself his tendency was to gamble—his

natural inclination. He was honest and true, poor fellow! Oh! has he no friend to keep him straight!'

'Hum! the friend that could have guided him, he couldn't get.'

'Still, I cannot—I will not blame myself. He has forgotten me long ago; and as I am sure I should have made him but a cold, unsympathetic wife, he might have gambled all the same, if I *had* married him. You are too cruel, Deb!'

'Ah! *grand Dieu!* Don't cry, my darlin'. You'll look a perfect fright, when your uncle comes! and, old or young, none of them have any feeling for an ill-looking woman. Besides, you are quite right. If the poor young man was a born gambler, maybe he would have beggared you. Do not think any more about him. You have done the flowers beautifully.'

'But I can't help thinking! I really liked Mr Waring. He had a fine nature in some ways, and oh! I do hope he is none the worse, really—for having met me.'

'Well, there is no use in troubling your head about him now?'

Mona made no reply, but she did not think the less.

Uncle Sandy arrived in a 'cawb,' and Madame Debrisay in her neat black dress—she never wore colours—and a pretty lace cap, went out to assist his descent from the vehicle. A sharp wrangle ensued over the fare, from which Mr Craig — cool, persistent, and utterly impervious to insult, where 'siller' was concerned—came forth triumphant.

Mona, who had been making sauce for the salad, according to Madame Debrisay's recipe, had just placed the salad bowl on the table, when he stumped in with the aid of stick and umbrella.

'Weel,' he said, tumbling into a chair and holding out his hand to Mona, 'I did not think I would live to see you again, but here I am.'

'You are looking better than I hoped to see you,' she said kindly.

'Eh! I have been awfu' bad, and I am varra lonely in yon place. Women-kind are aye thoughtful for the sick and weak, and I am pleased to take my bit dinner wi' you.'

'And we are glad to see you.'

'Can ye cook?' was his next question.

'Well, not much.'

'You see, my dear sir,' cried Madame Debrisay, 'the dear child has not much opportunity of learning; but she has a natural aptitude which I endeavour to cultivate.'

'That's right; every woman ought to cook. Ye see, that's their natural work, that and doctoring—I don't mean prescribing medicine, but seeing to its being swallowed.'

By this time dinner had been placed on the table, and Uncle Sandy appreciated a fried sole, some boiled fowl with white sauce, and a '*choufleur au gratin,*' prepared by Madame Debrisay's own and still pretty hands.

He spoke little while he ate, belonging to that unaffected class who think that dinner means eating—not social enjoyment.

VOL. I.   Q

When he had had enough, he pushed away his plate, and glancing at Madame Debrisay and Mona, who had been quietly waiting for him, returned thanks at some length, and then—very deliberately took a phial from his pocket, dropped a certain quantity into a glass, added water, and drank it.

'Ah!' he said, 'I have had a good dinner, which is conducive to digestion. Now, Mona, what is the meaning of that bit card in the window; is it to say the rooms are to let?'

'They are, uncle.'

'Then, if they are not too costly, I will take them. That young man—auld Robertson's son—has not behaved as he should, and it is as well I should have my brother's daughter to look after me.'

'I shall be very happy to do all I can for you, uncle; but you must remember that when my pupils come back to town, I shall be obliged to go out a great deal.'

'Never mind. Pupils or no pupils, you stick to me.'

Madame Debrisay gave a slight nod and a proud glance, expressing, 'Didn't I tell you,' most distinctly.

'I'll look after you, if you will look after me?' he continued. 'Whenever madame will come with me, I will go upstairs and see the place.'

This intention was duly carried out, and Uncle Sandy, after careful examination, pronounced all to be 'very good.'

'It would suit me weel to bide under the same roof with ye both' (he said 'baith'), 'and I do not wish to give any trouble. When ye buy for yersels, ye can buy for me. When ye have a pleasant book ye can lend it to me, and when I am frailer than my ordinair, she,' a nod to Mona, 'can read to me. Noo, I'll give a—I don't mind, twenty-five shillin' a week, for the twa rooms.'

'Let us see Mrs Puddiford,' quoth Madame Debrisay.

Whereupon a long discussion arose. Mr Craig had no objection to be a monthly tenant.

'I have let my wee place for two

years,' he said, 'and I can bide better here than elsewhere.'

So after some haggling, for he would not hear of looking elsewhere, he became Mrs Puddiford's tenant from the following Monday, at the large rent of five pounds ten per month.

END OF VOL. I.

COLSTON AND COMPANY, PRINTERS, EDINBURGH.

www.ingramcontent.com/pod-product-compliance
Lightning Source LLC
Chambersburg PA
CBHW022006050726
47499CB00006BB/1760